Rather Laugh than Cry

Rather Laugh Than Cry

Stories from a
Hassidic Household

MALKA ZIPORA

Véhicule Press

Published with the generous assistance of The Canada
Council for the Arts, the Book Publishing Industry
Development Program of the Department of Canadian
Heritage and the Société de développement des entreprises
culturelles du Québec (SODEC).

Cover photograph and design by Simon Garamond
Set in Mrs Eaves Roman by Simon Garamond
All drawings by the author
Published in French by Les Éditions du Passage
Printed by Marquis Book Printing Inc.

LIBRARY AND ARCHIVES CANADA CATALOGUING IN PUBLICATION
Zipora, Malka
Rather laugh than cry : stories from a Hassidic household
/ Malka Zipora.
ISBN 978-1-55065-220-8
1. Hasidim—Québec (Province)—Montréal—Social life and
customs—21st century.
2. Zipora, Malka—Family. I. Title.
FC2947.9.J4Z57 2007   305.6'9683320971428   C2007-900558-6

Published by Véhicule Press, Montréal, Québec, Canada
www.vehiculepress.com

Distribution in Canada by LitDistCo
orders@litdistco.ca

Distribution in U.S. by Independent Publishers Group
www.ipgbook.com

Printed in Canada on 100% post-consumer recycled paper.

This book is in memory of my dear mother, who was my biggest motivator. She lived with incredible wisdom, creativity and purity of soul, dedicating her life and energies to my father and to the children at the expense of denying herself the things her heart might have liked to pursue. Through my book, I feel that in some way I am fulfilling her aspirations and talent.

Contents

Preface

I originally wrote these stories for small magazines sold or distributed for my community. They covered issues that I discussed, laughed over or complained about with my friends as we sat on park benches nursing our babies, cleaning their faces of the sand they ate and threw at one another. In moments of inspiration, I would jot down my ideas on tissue boxes or make notes on junk mail while I stirred the soup. The stories were written for people like me, with similar backgrounds. My stories were tidbits of my life, with a fair amount of exaggeration for the benefit of a laugh.

Through what many might conceive as coincidence, they were destined (*bashert*) to spread to a wider and more diverse readership. I believe that the details surrounding the publication of the book, the events leading up to it, the characters involved in its inception and its publication were orchestrated by a Higher Hand. There were a series of events that *just so happened* to lead to a French publication of these stories in my book *Lekhaim*, translated by Pierre Anctil. Destiny (*bashert*) threw it onto my lap, and I took it as a message that it was G-d's will that this book should be published.

The success of the book and the warm and understanding reception from the public has encouraged me to publish an English version (the language in which it was originally written) and this is that book. When I wrote it, I took it for granted that the content was self-explanatory. That is until I met Nancy Marrelli, my publisher and editor—and very soon after—also my friend.

To the outsider Hassidic life is an enigma, so explanations or elaboration is required. In preparing the manuscript for publication I often heard the following mantra. "I don't know what you are talking about—you have to explain... EXPLAIN... EXPLAIN!" The process sometimes seemed like squeezing out the last bit of juice from a dried out lemon (that is me).

How could I possibly explain one's nature, faith and traditions—my DNA? Besides, why are such things of interest to others?

When I originally wrote in community magazines

about a story that happened on the Sabbath (*Shabbos*), I did not need to describe what Shabbos is all about. On Shabbos we feel as if we are on a different plane. The physical setting is different, as is the spiritual feeling: smelling the foods, singing the songs, discussions at the table, relaxing, feeling the euphoria of embracing the Sabbath at sundown, by lighting the candles with the family standing around waiting for the mother to take her hands from her eyes then calling out together *Gutt Shabbos*!, the kisses all around, and the tranquility that follows. A story is very different when it is a story written about an event on a Sabbath than if it were written about a weekday.

If I wrote about visiting someone in hospital on the Sabbath, my Hassidic readers would know the unwritten part was that I had walked two miles to the hospital, climbed eight floors of stairs and walked two miles back, because on the Sabbath it is forbidden to use transportation or take an elevator. Knowing this detail affects the reader's understanding of the story.

For a non-Hassidic reader, without explanation, the whole context of the story could be misunderstood. Trying to get the explanations into the flow of the story without losing its spontaneity is a challenge. I was reminded that many of the misconceptions and misunderstandings about Hassidic life exist precisely because there has been very little explanation from the source.

In many places I have included the Yiddish translation, when I felt that the word written in English did not arouse in me the same feelings that the Yiddish word did—the word was the closest I could get to the translation, or it needed some understanding and explanation. There are some additional explanations at the end of this book.

With these stories I have drawn aside the shades to the window in my home. What is exposed to the readers who care to look inside is not intended as a museum to the Hassidic way of life. Rather it provides glimpses of many universal emotions and stories. I am a Hassidic Mom, and I gingerly pull the curtains aside and invite you to peek inside and see things as they are. Please make allowances for the toys on the floor, and the cookie crumbs. It is impossible to be perfect.

I would like to express special thanks to my husband Joseph and my children who helped me with encouragement, feedback, and inspiration, making themselves available so that I could have time to write (and even more for allowing themselves to be the fodder for my stories).

Introduction

I am a Hassidic Mom.

As a child, I used to lie in bed and design my life. I would marry the perfect man, a scholar with a gentle character, and be a mother with one hundred children who were beautiful, talented, clever, always clean and well-behaved. In my custom-designed life I could afford whatever I desired. I did a lot of dreaming, because dreams were about all my parents could afford.

With the notion of destiny (*bashert*) so ingrained into my faith, I knew that despite my dreams, my future was already destined from Above. How I would handle my destiny and the choices I would make were up to me. A person thinks, and G-d laughs (*a mentch tracht und der aibishter lacht*) at our naiveté.

With our limitations, a human being can only see

the small picture that relates to one's own personal world as one sees it. There is a much larger all-encompassing picture out there, where each person's life fits in like a piece of a puzzle. Though the big picture is far too complex to fully understand, I see and feel the Guiding Hand more clearly as the years go by.

I married the scholar of good and gentle character, and I was surprised to discover that that was not what made a marriage. Relationships are not handed out on a golden platter but must be developed and built, and this requires investment. Having my dream fulfilled was not enough. It was much easier to design a husband than to customize myself to be the wife of *his* dreams. The children began coming within a year, and the challenges that come with raising children was a crash course in developing a relationship. The greatest undertaking in the world—raising a generation of children—requires teamwork, commitment and the physical and moral support of both partners if we are to do it right. I have learned more about human nature and relationships through raising my children than I ever could have studied in a hundred years.

Instead of my one hundred children, I only had twelve and these children did get dirty, they got sick and needed their teeth fixed. They argued, kept me up nights, and when I wanted to show off, I was surprised to find there were other children as beautiful, as talented, and as clever as mine, and they were often even better behaved.

Neither did my financial destiny match my grandiose dreams. I still check the weekly grocery flyers for the specials of the week, and plan my menus according to the specials. The challenges have added a richness that I could never have imagined or have appreciated while I was wrapped up in my dreams.

I live, metaphorically speaking, with the shades down, for the light in our home comes from within. Home is sacred, and all values stem from there. Home is where we nurture our physical, emotional and spiritual welfare. Home is our history, and the preparation for a future that follows a well-trodden path, in the footsteps of my parents.

My parents were Hungarian Holocaust survivors who escaped to a land where they could breathe freely, and where they were treated well. They brought the "home" of their parents with them to new shores.

They were able to survive those years of living hell by measuring their self worth according to the strength of the values they learned from home.

Even when they lived under subhuman conditions, where "swine" (*swein*) became their first name in the concentration camps, they did not sway from their traditions. Their attitude to their captors was fear and revulsion, never envy. Rather, they envied the birds that flew overhead in freedom. If the most civilized of humanity could rationalize genocide, infanticide, and killing the sick and disabled as an honorable goal, it only served to intensify my parents' determination and commitment to their old ways. My father ate only kosher at a time when food was rationed below the minimum. He traded away his one slice of bread a day for a sugar cube, which he saved for Passover, when leavened bread is forbidden according to Jewish law. He hid his phylactories (*tefillin*) and little prayer book (*siddur*) praying with them under a blanket before anyone woke up. His drive to preserve the traditions was his incentive and purpose to live.

My mother was only fourteen when her world turned upside down, but those fourteen years set the guidelines for the rest of her life. "That is how it was at home (*udj volt othon*)," she used to say, and she meant that was how things should be. Those first fourteen years were only one fifth of her life.

The walls of our childhood homes are the fortresses where we preserve and practice our traditions. Each Hassidic home is unique, yet every home has very much in common. I know what the menu is at every ceremonial meal (*seuda*) in a Hassidic house on the Sabbath

(*Shabbos*). When I hear through the open window, my neighbor's family singing a particular melody, I know which course is being served next. From the tunes (*nigun*) of the traditional songs (*zemiros*) I can identify from which part of Europe the grandfather emanated, or at which yeshiva he must have studied. History is part of our daily ritual.

A combination of a code of laws (*halacha*) and traditions cover every aspect of our day from the minute we open our eyes, even before we step out of bed, until we fall asleep. A truly Hassidic house is devoid of any external influences such as public media, whose entertainment prevails at the cost of values. The sources of inspiration are the family unit, the Talmud and those scholars who invest themselves into its study, and the men and women who spend their lives doing kindness (*chesed*) to others. The stories and traditions passed on (*mesora*) from father to son, from rabbis to students, from a mother to her children, relate all the way back to Mount Sinai. They are a window to our past.

It takes a conscious effort and struggle to sidestep the lure of modern times, where many traditions and values that were once universally preserved are no longer celebrated. Once we leave the confines of our homes we are greeted with stark contrasts. Against this backdrop of modern life, the Hassid withdraws, and to those unaccustomed to their ways, appears like a holdover from a forgotten era, an anachronism.

As a wife and mother, I have invested all my resources into building a warm environment that can withstand the driving elements of change. I feel blessed to see a continuation of the values our children grew up with integrated into their own homes. This enables my husband and me to share and understand their experiences, and we continue to be very much a part of their lives after they have made their own.

My home vibrates with intensity and emotion. It is a passionate life. Tears are an expression of passion. Tears of sorrow and tears of joy often flow together. The greatest joy has an element of sadness, and in the greatest sadness, one can find joy. This can be explained with an analogy to a prince being crowned a king. On the happiest day of his life when he succeeds to the crown, he also mourns his father's death.

Joy is a heavenly gift, and those who are in that state have the power to bless others. That is why, when we are in our most joyful state—such as celebrating a birth or a wedding—we make a conscious effort to remember those who suffer. Only by feeling the sorrow of others are we truly able to bless them. That is why troubled people will write their names and their requests to G-d, be it for health, sustenance, or finding a partner in life, and give it to the bride or groom to pray for them. That is why the tears can flow under the wedding canopy one minute—and a minute later, the faces of the newlyweds radiate with smiles.

Humor helps us blend the joy and sorrow. Humor reveals many truths without hurting, boosts relationships, and brings joy and good feeling. Humor can show up our failings, and help us accept them or improve them. It plays a huge part in Hassidic life, balancing many dimensions of our life. Humor is celebrated, and it enables one to *rather laugh than cry*. Humor has helped me celebrate moments of chaos that come with a houseful of children with more energy than I, and laugh at such times, instead of crying.

The Red Pants

I sit on the floor, surrounded by a mountain of boxes. The snow outside has melted. Passover (*Pesach*) is approaching, and with it comes the new season, which means preparing the children's winter wardrobe. I wade into the contents of the boxes to sort out the clothing accumulated over the years. I must decide the fate of each item; which child will inherit it this year, or put it aside to review again next season, or get rid of it altogether. It is an emotionally exhausting occupation, for these clothes are saturated with vivid and sentimental memories.

I stare lovingly at the little red pants at the top of the pile. They have outlived the store where I purchased them over twenty years ago. I remember how the little outfit taunts me for three days begging me from the window—"Buy me! Buy me!" The price is marked just above the fancy European label. Never before have I spent the exorbitant price of *sixteen dollars* on a child's outfit. My conscience and I are at war.

"Just this once!" I reason with myself. "Little Moishy will look royal. His black hair and eyes against the red fabric."

Yes, it is obvious that the outfit is destined for me...or is it? Why not?

"Can I justify spending so much, when my budget is so tight?" I ask myself. "Maybe if I save on diapers by changing them less often? No? Okay, I won't spend on treats for a half a year.... Of course I can afford it! I deserve it ... I can ... I will! ... And before the next objection can arise I run into the store, leaving my conscience outside to watch the carriage. This is how the little red pants come to be intertwined with the history of my family.

Moishy is irresistible. I walk him, wheel him and parade him, strutting proudly, confident that crowds are lining up to see the remarkable Moisheleh (little Moishy) in his red pants. I try to stifle my disdain for anyone who does not dress his or her children as well as I do.

I hem the pants up one season and down the next, so that the next child can use them. Sheindl, unlike Moishy, is chubby and blond. Her blue eyes sparkle and she fills the red pants to the maximum-plus. Her natural bulges are advertised by the contour-hugging double knit. She is adorable and I have long forgotten the price. The compliments keep coming despite the evident hemlines.

And it comes to pass that Avromeleh (little Avraham) is heir to the outfit. He does not share my respect for it, and his persistent crawling thins out the knees of the red pants. The thread I use to mend it is so close in colour that one really has to make an effort to notice it. My favorite picture of Benyamin (the next in line) shows him smiling happily in the exact same red pants in all their glory.

It may have been somewhere between Leah and Yoel—I do not remember which child wore the outfit—when one of the eyes of the embroidered giraffe disappears. It does not matter, for the charm remains. I think it is cute when I change the matching knit shirt for one that is less frayed, though not quite so perfectly matched. For Yoel I add fancy patches at the knees and fool the whole world into thinking that they belong to the original design of the pants. I do not notice that the compliments stopped long ago. Nevertheless, I am sure that this is exactly the finery that every mother would wish for her child.

As I sort through the winter clothes, I sit reflecting for fifteen minutes, debating whether the time is ripe to hand the pants down to Lipa. The truth is, I am not so desperate, because over the years I have sporadically bought quite a few more 'memories', which I will get to as soon as I have decided on the destiny of these red pants.

The door opens and I am caught red handed, (or red pantsed) by my daughter Sheindl, now all grown up, who has accomplished quite a bit of Passover (Pesach) cleaning while I am meditating. She stares at the red pants.

"Mummy, you're not keeping that rag (shmatteh) ...or are you?" she bursts out in disbelief. "Half those boxes should have been dumped long ago" she says pointing to the stack that almost reaches the ceiling.

"A rag? What heresy!" I think to myself, but I know I am defeated. Without the memories, that is exactly what the red pants are—rags!

I cannot bear to part so abruptly with this emotional treasure, so I suggest giving it away to charity (gemach).

"O h p l e a s e, Mummy! They would be embarrassed to wear this in Rwanda. Anyway, I need a good rag to wipe the top of the china cabinet."

I stare at her wordlessly, feeling misunderstood. How could she be so disloyal to something that had served her so well eighteen years ago? So, this is what is meant by the generation gap!

Sheindl rips the pants apart and marches off with

two limp red cloths that had once been full and bursting with little Sheindl herself. Dutifully, with one goal in mind, she hurries to polish the furniture with my precious memories.

Bedtime Tale

Combining the role of writer and mother is like swimming upstream. As soon as I come up with some prodigious idea to write about, there is a tidal wave of activity in my house. I try to turn the tide, and my train of thought takes a totally different turn. Alternating between the typewriter, dentist appointments and listening to my children pour out their hearts about classroom politics is quite a challenge. What compounds my difficulty in coordinating an article with mediating arguments, is that illusionary phenomenon we call ' bedtime.'

Whatever happened to those days when at 7 p.m. I could hear a pin drop? I could relax, or prepare for the next day, or do those myriad things I could not get around to doing during the day. I actually had the luxury of *thinking* without interruption. Once upon a time, I was queen of my castle and my word was law. Any offspring out of bed after the first flicker of the street lamp had to have a good excuse. Nothing short of an earthquake or volcanic eruption would suffice.

Today, the children don't need sleep. With maternal warmth, every evening I go through the bedtime motions, donning pyjamas, saying bedtime prayers, goodnight greetings and tender kisses, then the waltz into bed. Either a fool or an optimist by nature, I naively assume that after this routine the night will be mine. Then, as I pick up the pieces and unscramble the socks from the toy box, I hear the first patter of feet heading for the sink.

"I'm thirsty."

Suddenly everyone's kidneys go into overdrive, and there is a line up in front of the facilities. A quick calculation reveals that the amount of water consumed, plus the flushing and hand washing roughly equals half the contents of the St. Lawrence River flowing down my drain each evening.

No matter how securely I tuck the little darlings into bed, the beds conspire to eject their inhabitants. I am barely out of the room before the bedsprings are transformed into trampolines, and the room becomes a circus ring of acrobatic performers.

When I am asked about the number of children I

have, I must first ascertain whether they are referring to a.m. or p.m., because in the evening hours my family multiplies tenfold. At bedtime, I can discover the same child simultaneously in thirteen different places. I must admit, I feel outnumbered.

I sweep the spilled glitter, tear off the red construction paper that is glued to the sole of my shoes, and prepare for Bedtime Olympics. Chaya initiates the ceremonies with an important message.

"Shloimeh needs the bathroom."

Please understand, that Shloimeh is in the process of being trained, and timing is of the essence. My palpitations almost knock me over as I run accompanied by an entourage of cheering mini people all anxious to witness the outcome of the drama. Would I make it on time? Would Shloimeh?

We don't! Then I start the bedtime manoeuvres all over again. By now, it is somewhere between 9.30 p.m. and 11.00 p.m. and all the chronic ailments surface— stomach aches, headaches, earaches, toe cramps.... The exorbitant number of limbs possessed by the human species is mind-boggling.

Though I have read many books on child rearing, I cannot remember anyone addressing the issue of why children can whine for food all day, yet are never hungry at mealtimes. At that time food becomes sport, playdough, a catapult or facial cream. It is never ingested. Interestingly, as soon as the word "pajamas" is uttered, their metabolisms accelerate and my children turn into a starving horde.

Unlike adults, whose minds deteriorate by the hour, children operate in the reverse mode. Their memories recharge and display instant recall as the hour draws closer to midnight.

"Mummy, you said we could play with the puzzle after supper!"

"Yesterday you said we could bake cupcakes after school!"

"I did not review my homework, and the teacher said I will get a red mark if I don't."

"Why can't camels fly?"

I beg, I cajole. I make new promises.

"Tomorrow there will be time for cupcakes. "

" I'll have the teacher fired if she dares give a red mark."

"Sunday we will go bumper car racing. "

"Camels can't fly, because the mother camel would never be able to get the babies into bed."

"I will give you the moon" and as a last resort...

"*When I count to three you all better be in bed!*" My facial features become threatening.

One day, I will challenge myself not to enforce bedtime. Shloimeh will doze off in the high chair. Leah will be bent over her bed hugging her doll. Chaya will retire to her corner sucking her thumb. Benyomin will fall asleep with a book... Then I will gently creep up with the pyjamas in my hand. Deep in my heart, I know that the minute I do this, my house will teem again with nightlife. My little army will march back and forth from bedroom to bathroom to kitchen and back, and we will be wishing each other goodnight until the break of dawn.

Alarmed

I hang up the phone with a friend after she yawns for the third time, assuming she is gently hinting that the conversation is boring. Somewhat humiliated, I turn to commiserate with my husband, who barely refrains from yawning as he listens. Later that day, I ask the cashier at the grocery store, where to find a certain item. With a bleary-eyed look he smothers a yawn, and says as if it is his last breath.

"At the end of the aisle, to the left...*a a a a h o o uh*"

Only when I catch myself regularly stretching and yawning, do I realize that these gestures are not personal insults, but rather a sign of the times. My gut feeling tells me that fatigue is a by-product of the invention of the alarm clock.

Alarm clocks are the root of all evil. They mess up our instinctive time awareness, so we feel it is way past bedtime from the moment we wake. I owe the bags under my eyes to this menace to humanity.

The perfect alarm clock was designed on the fourth day of creation, in the form of a rooster. This amazing fowl was programmed to announce sunrise, without a snooze button. Unlike most of us, the rooster celebrates the break of dawn by crowing. It crows long enough to give no more than a five-minute chance to turn over and catch an extra few winks. The sound is pleasant but if it does bother anyone, a stone thrown in the rooster's direction would set it crowing to someone else, who hopefully would be more receptive. Whoever is presumptuous enough to try to improve on this magnificent creation should have an alarm installed permanently into his/her ear canal.

With a house full of early rising young scholars (*bochurim*) I have alarm clocks set at every corner of the house. Six weeks in winter are dedicated to intensive study and repentance (*shovevim*), when these young men awake even earlier than their usual pre-dawn waking time on Friday morning. That is when the house resembles a fire station.

Beginning from 4:30 a.m. each boy's timepiece is scheduled to ring at half hour intervals. Moishy has become so immune to the sound of one clock that he has added another to the shelf, as a backup. His brother Avrohom makes a deal with his sister who will also set her alarm 'just in case'. On top of that, they forge agreements with their study partners (*chevruso*) that the first to get out of bed will make a telephone call to wake the other. There is no lack of creativity. A foolproof system has been developed.

Four o'clock in the morning and the alarms start to detonate. Moishy's day is scheduled to start at four thirty, leaving him a half-hour for snooze time. His brother, due to wake at five, sleepily implores him to turn it off. His petition falls on deaf ears, because Moishy's head is buried in the blanket to tune out all sound.

I am the kind of mother who keeps abreast of what happens within the house, even in my sleep. In fact I even once overheard my little Leah, telling her siblings "Mummy never sleeps, she just lies with her eyes closed." I am vigilant from the first ring, ready to step forward in case the wake up system should collapse. Precisely when I hear the splash of his morning ablutions (*negel vasser*) prepared near his bed, is when Avraham's alarm begins to chime.

Avraham, who has lost a half-hour of precious sleep coaxing his brother to switch off his alarm and wake up, now requires a half-hour of peace. He snoozes his button for a few repeats, to the chorus of his younger brother, Benyamin's *"Shush!,"* which is one or two tones louder than the alarm. Benyamin has one hour before it is his time to rise.

I cannot relegate motherhood to a time slot. Throughout the pre-dawn commotion, I toss and turn. My bed becomes hot coals and with my eye glued to my clock, I wait "patiently" before I intervene. I empathize with Benyamin's interrupted sleep, and I am very concerned that Avraham should be on schedule. I allow myself until one second after five before I step in. The moment my toe touches the floor I hear Avraham wash. I spring back into bed, but the peace is short lived. Benyamin is drained by his efforts to get Avraham to switch off the alarm, and as soon as Avraham is up, Benyamin dozes off. His timing is precisely two minutes before the eruption of his TWO alarms, which are set for one half hour earlier than his waking time.

I was once violently awakened from a deep sleep, by a crowd of people crying amid desperate calls for help. "Help! Save me! Save me!" (*Rattevet! Rattevett!*) My pounding heart almost knocks me over, and my adrenaline-infused blood impels me to race to the room from which the commotion emanates. I burst into Benyamin's room, praying to find him alive. Benyamin is sound asleep. Near his bed, six inches from his eardrum is a cassette recorder set to a timer, on maximum volume, playing a tape of his Rebbe, with

his awe inspiring holiday (*Hoshana Rabba*) suppli-
cations. Surely an inspirational tape like that, which
moved thousands to tears of repentance (*teshuvai*)
should be able to wake up Benyamin, in more ways
than one!

My eyeballs roll around in coordination with the
second hand on my clock as Benyamin keeps pressing
the snooze button. Five minutes...ten minutes....
fifteen minutes and thirty two seconds. I run to wake
him, just as he splashes *his* first round of ablutions
(*negel vasser*). The baby cries, and the moon disappears, signalling the start of a new day. I start the new
day with a yawn.

Zay Matsliach

True fulfillment is the feeling one gets for doing something of value. Not always do we see the immediate results of our efforts. Usually we never know the ripple effects of our actions. Believing our conduct has an effect inspires us to do worthwhile acts with or without self-gratification. As humans, our knowledge and understanding is limited to our own personal universe of facts, feelings, prejudices and emotions. There is no gauge to measure the true value of every deed.

Our sages advise us in *Ethics of our Fathers* (*Pirkei Avos*) to "Run to accomplish a small good deed, just as you would run to something difficult (and therefore more obvious and more admirable)" for the accounting in Heaven is not exactly as we imagine, and the value of even a small deed stretches farther than we can imagine. Magnanimous acts of great unusual courage or selflessness are noticed, commended and admired. That smaller kind deeds go unnoticed does not negate their value.

Ten years ago I rated the importance of my daily greetings as somewhere between brushing teeth and making school lunches. Then I began to realize as the children grew, and as the relationship between my husband and myself developed, that the accumulation of little gestures and deeds has lasting effects.

With time, the morning exchange of greetings and wishing everybody to 'be successful' (*zay matsliach*) has become part of our daily ritual. This all-encompassing blessing imparted with all my love, includes also the things taken for granted, from crossing the streets safely, to hoping that every endeavor will turn out well. This sendoff breaks the morning inertia, and leaves me feeling that my day has started purposefully.

It is six in the morning, and the day has officially begun. The bigger boys (*bochurim,*), Avraham and Benyamin are leaving for the academy (*yeshiva*). They rummage around in the refrigerator for their breakfasts and lunches that were prepared the night before. I have begged them many times to at least whisper "have a good day" (*a guten tug*) as they pass my room, thus giving me the opportunity to wish them "be successful."

Just two words invested with warm feelings and good will that will subliminally affect their attitude to their Torah learning and their surroundings throughout the day. Fearing to wake me, they wordlessly slip by my room on tiptoes.

My extra sensory perception operates at all hours. I quickly call out *"zay matsliach!"* with my closed eyes before they close the front door.

By quarter to eight Yoel and Shloimeh leave. I spend some time together with them over breakfast, and part from them with my trademark *zay matsliach*, wrapped in a current of inner emotion. The two brothers travel the same route each with their own individual thoughts and feelings. They will subconsciously process my *zay matsliach* and incorporate these wishes to fit in with their own little world. I cannot tell them all the things that they will need to know. I cannot deny them the lessons brought about by experience, but maybe my *zay matsliach* sendoff is a subconscious route to draw their hearts to me, letting them know that I am an ally when crossroads come their way.

These words are a buttress to balance the many times when I must tell them what they do not want to hear, such as "That is not acceptable" or even worse— "No!" When I warmly wish them *zay matsliach*, I am also telling them I love them and wish them well, even when I set limitations.

Then the girls, Leah, Chaya and Raizy begin leaving for work and for school. Girls tend to share their emotions and experiences more than boys usually do (and often slightly more than I wish to know). They leave me with a *zay matsliach* on my lips and my head spinning with their stories or issues. I hope they will resolve their little burdens, and pray that the new ones should only be minor ones, like resolvable relationships with friends and co-workers, bothersome pimples, or walking in the cold... The morning departures and greetings continue with tempo. My morning *zay matsliachs*, intended to perk up their day, also give me a lift.

I make a mental note of all the things I want to discuss with my husband Joseph who, in the fifteen-minute interval between two school buses, arrives home from synagogue before he leaves for work. My planned discussions rarely materialize, because he is busy with Shulem, the baby who is due for a feeding, while I am trying to coax another spoonful into his brother Lipa's mouth, before he leaves for school.

Getting the children ready on time takes priority, and Shulem does not understand that he must be patient for a few minutes. Under such circumstances conversation between Joseph and myself are limited to shouting stilted sentences over the baby's cries.

"Where is the pacifier?"

"Just rock him while I tie Lipa's shoes."

"I called the plumber to fix the blocked sink. Will you be home after twelve?"

The most personal our conversation gets is when he leaves for the day. We make our parting greetings at the door, after which I call out one more time, *zay matsliach!*, as he walks down the steps. He understands those words as deeply as I do.

Lipa's bus comes next. He waves to his father, who leaves a few minutes before the bus arrives, yelling repeatedly through the closed window. "Bye Tatti! Bye!" Joseph must walk backwards and continue waving uninterrupted until he turns the corner, or else Lipa will throw a tantrum that "Tatti did not say 'Bye'" and stubbornly refuse to go to school until "Tatti says 'Bye!'" At such times I make an exhibit of myself as the world's most wicked mother, physically dumping her child on the waiting school bus, while he screams "Tatti did not say 'Bye!'"

Sometimes miracles occur and the baby is fed and dressed, and so am I with time to spare before Lipa's bus comes. In this case, we wait for the bus together. As soon as the bus leaves I go to settle errands with Shulem in the carriage. I leave the residue of the morning "hurricane" for later. Otherwise, if I clean up the mess, then the baby will nap until the rest of the children will come home, and I will miss the opportunity to do errands without the rest of my "kinder-garten" tagging along.

The panorama, as I watch it with Lipa behind the window, reveals many stories. Men in black coats and hats walk back and forth from the different synagogues with their embroidered prayer shawl bags under their arms. The ones without the bags are leaving home to go to work. Some wives work outside the home, and they or their husbands wheel baby carriages to their parents/in-laws/ babysitters. Some men have already started their business day even before reaching home after morning prayers. Their arms flail as they speak on their cell phones, and one can see by the intensity of their motions if their wives are asking them to run into the bakery for milk and bread, or whether a shipment they ordered did not arrive on time.

The topography tells me how to dress Lipa. I can detect the approximate temperature outside by the appearance of the street. When the road is light gray, and the snow on the sidewalk is firm and crystalline, then the weather is biting cold. Icicles hang like a valance of daggers from the balconies, indicating that the weather had originally been warmer but became cold again. Sunshine in winter as seen from behind glass gives the illusion of warmth. I have learned by now, the clearer and sunnier the sky, the more I must bundle up the children.

I measure the velocity of the wind by the way the scarves flap, and I familiarize myself with neighbors whose children go to different schools. I have also become a sort of mechanic—with Lipa as my teacher. He recognizes the details that distinguish one school bus from another. Identifying the distinguishing lights of Lipa's school bus from afar gives me advance notice to go downstairs.

From behind the window I observe without being observed, and I make a sociological study of how different mothers relate to their children as they wait for their buses. They range from the perfectionists who regularly adjust the hood and the scarf to cover any exposed inch of skin, to protect the child from the biting cold, or the mother who will run together with the child, boots and jacket in hand and dress the child on the step of the bus. I have picked out my favorite bus monitors and drivers according to how they greet the children as they get onto the buses.

Lipa and I have a wait- for-the-bus-game guessing how many cars will pass before his bus arrives. The best guess wins. Though I can read a clock, I usually give him a chance to win by making drastic over-estimations. As we play, Lipa shares tidbits of his life.

He picks and chooses what he likes from the things I say, some things to be utilized immediately and some things will be conserved in the archives of his being, to be restored later in life. He will most probably forget this moment, or lump it in the archives of his memory with all the other mundane Mummy talk, but I still like to believe that these conversations are building blocks to a relationship that will open doors between us and allow me to offer guidance, inspiration or just positive feelings in the future.

The bus turns the corner and he races down. "*Zay matsliach!*" I yell as the door opens. The tassel on his hat swings irregularly as he clumsily runs with his boots clomping over a snowy hill, scarf flapping "goodbye" to me from behind him. With lunchbox in one hand and shoe bag in the other hand Lipa maneuvers himself onto the big step of the bus, before the monitor can help him up.

"*Zay matsliach!*" I yell just before the bus door closes. Lipa never looks back; he is intent on getting to his seat before the bus gives a jerk. "*Zay matsliach!*" I mumble once more to no one and everyone, as I close my door and venture into the routine of my day.

I have offered them a crutch to balance the slippery slide of growing up. I cannot know how much or how little these "Mommy words" mean to him, but for me they are crucial.

One small telephone call from Raizy at school convinces me to trust my intuition that greetings are never in vain.

"Mummy, you were on the phone when I left, and we couldn't... um, say.... I am soon having a test...." and she giggles her trademark giggle of awkwardness.

What she is trying to say is that I did not wish her *zay matsliach* this morning and she is embarrassed to admit that such a trivial thing is so important to her, but she feels they will make a difference to the outcome of her test.

"*Zay matsliach!*" I tell her with all my heart. Her responsive giggle indicates that she is glad I take her seriously, for those words are meaningful to her.

"Thanks Mummy, *zay matsliach!*"

May the day be successful! I do not take a minute for granted. G-d (*Hashem*) Thank you for everything.

Challah for the Sabbath

There is nothing so heartwarming as coming home on Friday afternoon, with the smell of challah baking in the oven. I remember it vividly when I was a child. Today I am the one baking the challah. I relive the childhood pleasure when my family, or whoever enters my house, never fails to comment: "Mmm, smells delicious."

Fresh challah is always delicious, but challah on the Sabbath is never the same as challah during the week. The sanctity and the spirit of the Sabbath add an extra ingredient to all the food, but especially to the challah. It is the highlight of the Sabbath meal, eaten with or dipped into the salads or sauces, or just nibbled on throughout the meal.

There is something extra special about our own

mother's challah. Everyone remembers his or her mother's challah as something very special. My mother spoke of her mother's challah as if the golden loaves were world-renowned masterpieces, and I in turn thought there was no other challah like my mother's. My children make delicious challah of their own, but I beam with pride when they talk about my challah as if it were manna sent from heaven. There is an unwritten understanding that is as unchangeable as the Constitution, that if Mother did it that way—that is the only right way. There is something almost spiritual about challah from "home."

One young mother, who has been making challah for years, never forgets to cut a little off the ends of the braided challah before putting it in the pan. When asked why she does this, she points to her mother, who makes her challah the self-same way. Ask her mother why she did this, and she points in turn to her mother who never fails to cut the ends before baking.

"Why do I cut my challah?" her mother repeats my question as I wait with bated breath for some great story from folklore. "Why shouldn't I cut it?"

Besides buying time, answering one question with another question has the added benefit of building up the intrigue.

"So you have no particular reason?" I ask, bracing myself for a revelation.

"Well, what else should I do, if my baking pans are too small?" She answers with a hint of condescension for not grasping the obvious.

A challah recipe is only a guideline, because baking challah is really a relationship between the dough and its maker. When making the dough, I gloat as I watch it grow and breathe. Just like plants respond to the heart of the planter, the more attention one gives, the more it flourishes, so too does the dough respond to tender loving care.

The following is my personal challah recipe in case you should want to try your hand at it. It changes according to the dynamics of the home. However, I must add that the main ingredient that makes the challah so special is the Sabbath itself.

➢Sixteen cups (six pounds) all purpose flour finely sifted into a large mixing bowl.
Run to put pacifier into baby's mouth every four cups.

➢Three ounces yeast to which you add one cup of room temperature water and one tablespoon sugar. Leave until fermentation begins and bubbles begin to appear
Don't answer the telephone if it should happen to ring— you might forget to add the sugar.

➤Add to the flour nine tablespoons sugar and two tablespoons salt. Mix it up well so the salt does not prevent the yeast from fermenting.

*Answer everyone's questions **before** you do this, or you risk adding two spoons sugar and nine of salt by mistake.*

➤Five cups of water at room temperature.

Place the water in the middle of the table so if your audience wishes to help you bake, or stands on a chair for a better position, the water should be seen and not hurled.

➤Mix two eggs with two tablespoons less than half a cup of oil.

If the doorbell rings, let them wait!

➤Make a well in the middle of the flour and spill in the egg and oil mixture.

*Wash the hands of your helper who just dipped his/her finger into the well. Do not stop kneading once you begin adding liquids. If you **must** take a telephone call, support the phone between your head and shoulders. Contact your physiotherapist for an appointment after your challah-making is completed.*

➤Add the five cups water and mix it well.

At this point it is essential to keep your hands in the bowl. Don't wave them around to emphasize a point— knives are dangerous. Keep your mind on what you are doing—the dough might fall on the floor and slipping on it is dangerous. If you grab a child who is about to fall from a viewing perch, remember that dough is adhesive and the two of you are likely to become permanently bonded.

➤Knead for about five or six minutes or until the texture is well blended, soft and rubbery. Cover loosely with a clean plastic bag that has been lightly oiled, making sure there is room in the bowl for the dough to grow. Keep the dough away from drafts—a nice warm spot is good. Let it rise about an hour or until it is almost double in size.

*Use this time to pick up pieces of stray dough, apologize to the kids for whatever you said while you were knead- ing, bathe one child, and call in your grocery order. Refer to your husband anyone in your vicinity who wants something from you or needs anything in the next three hours. He is just as capable and probably more patient. You may also have time to convince your son who claims that size fourteen is too small for him (and there are no clean shirts in the closet that fit him), that he **is** size fourteen, at least until the challah is done.*

➤Uncover the dough, punch it down and knead it for two minutes. One sign of well-risen dough is that there are many small holes in a piece that has been cut off. *I separate a small piece of dough and make a blessing dedicating it to G-d. This is not for consumption— it is eventually placed in the oven and left to burn to ashes.*

➤Cut the dough into preferred sizes. Fill the baking pans only three quarters full to allow space for the challah to expand. I make four rolls, three small loaves and three larger loaves.

➤Knead each piece into a ball one at a time and cut the ball into equal pieces—four, or six, depending upon how many strands you will use to braid the challah. Roll each piece into a long strip.

➤Braid the long strips as artistically as you can.

➤Beat an egg lightly and add a teaspoon sugar, then brush each loaf with the mixture using a pastry brush. Leave to rise for about half an hour after finishing all the braiding. *Use this time to apologize again for saying the things you apologized for earlier and as a gesture of recon- ciliation find some reason to say "wow!" or "that's great!" to each person who was ignored or who was too well noticed.*

➤Smear dough again with the egg mixture, and sprinkle with sesame or poppy seeds.

➤Place baking pans in an **un-preheated** oven. Set temperature to 350° and bake for about one hour. Remove loaves from pans and bake on the racks for another 15 minutes. Small loaves and rolls should bake for about 45 minutes in the pans before a final fifteen minutes out of the pan.

Recruit everyone to help clean up and prepare for Sabbath. Let the "shoe shine" boy or girl line up all the shoes for polishing. The "candle man" must prepare the candles on the trays with the candelabras, fill the oil burners with olive oil and wicks, stick the candles into the holders by slightly melting them. The big ones bathe the little ones. The "messenger boy or girl" must be on hand to run every two minutes to buy whatever you forgot to order—diapers, tissues, water....The "electrician" makes sure that all timers are adjusted to your needs, and switches are taped up or down—because on Sabbath there is no changing electrical settings. The "dry goods department" sees that the Sabbath clothes are prepared; the pockets are emptied of anything not permitted on Sabbath, such as money; and any buttons that need fixing must be done in advance; fresh towels and tablecloths, and flowers in the vase. The "vacuumer" does the vacuuming, the table must be set, the goblets polished. When the challahs are ready two large ones are set at the head of the table and covered with an embroidered tablecloth. *Gut Shabbos!*

ENJOY!

Leave the challah to rise

A Fishy Story

My mother-in-law once remarked that when her children rubbed their stomachs at mealtime, ostensibly demonstrating their gustatory delight, she knew that the meal would soon draw to a close. After another two or three spoonfuls (if she was lucky), the meal was over. Neither bribe nor threat could move her children to finish what was left on their plates.

I too have certain formulas that have proven true over time. I pass these truisms on to my now married children. They listen dutifully enough, but I know, however, that it will take real-life experience of their very own for them to become true believers.

One of these principles goes as follows: whenever a child wants something very badly and whines and begs for it, *the very moment the parent caves in,* the object of desire depreciates in value. Desire and fulfillment are somehow inextricably related. Our Sages knew this quirk of human nature and they taught. "Stolen waters are sweet," (*Mayim genuvim yimtaku*). Only in my case, the waters included the fishy kind. I am talking about the time ten-year-old Sheindl longed and pined for a goldfish; this was soon exacerbated into a desperate *need* to have a goldfish.

It starts when Sheindl's friend Raizy buys a goldfish. Raizy regales an avid audience with the adventures of her fish. Details are provided in proportion to the audience's attention. Sheindl certainly pays attention. There is only a short distance between Sheindl's wouldn't-it-be-nice-to-have-a-fish phases until the I-MUST-HAVE-GOLDFISH-OTHERWISE-LIFE-IS-NOT-WORTH-LIVING phase. This evolution takes place in *less than an hour*. In fact, it happens during the very hour in which I bathe the little ones and cajole them into pajamas.

To realize her desires, Sheindl faces one major obstacle—me. Instinctively Sheindl trains her finely-honed persuasive tactics on me.

Now, I have nothing against goldfish. I am a nature lover, albeit from a respectful distance, but long ago I decided that dealing with twelve of G-d's creatures, made in His very own image, living in my very own home is just as much as I could handle, thank you.

"It must be fun to have a goldfish. Goldfish are so nice to watch," my daughter muses pointedly, as I sort the laundry. With her elbow on the windowsill, she gazes out dreamily at the world, watching for my reaction from the corner of her eye.

"Mmmm" I agree innocently. After all, I also enjoy watching the fish—the ones in my dentist's aquarium, that is.

Somewhat encouraged, Sheindl proceeds to the next step.

"Raizy, has a goldfish, and she l-o- v-e-s it," she says, as I peel carrots.

"That must be nice," I agree with a smile. "For Raizy." I add quickly.

Sheindl is quiet, but only for a minute. I have a chilly sense of foreboding.

"If only..." Sheindl's eyes are directed hopefully, longingly, at some point on the ceiling.

This is where I begin to slide. I do not react assertively. I do not even buy time with my usual I-have-to-think-about-this line. Instead, I say, somewhat lamely, "But we don't have anywhere to keep goldfish."

Sheindl is well prepared.

"There's room on the top of my bedroom dresser," She says quickly.

Sarcasm, it is said, is the defense of the weak. If that were true, I am definitely getting punier each second.

"Sure," I say. "The goldfish will have a grand time wading through your books, clothes and all the rest of the stuff that sits on your dresser from one Sabbath to the next."

Now here is some simple advice to all you parents out there: Get a lawyer. Otherwise, anything you say will be held against you. (Not only will your listener use your words to outsmart you, *you* will soon regret anything you say other than NO! Nyet! Nem! Non! Nein! or No in any language you may speak.) But, this is not the kind of wisdom I am privy to at the time.

Sheindl is soon suffused with the kind of hope a surprised victor must feel. "Mummy, you will *see*, if I *only* had a goldfish, *everything* will be different. There will be *nothing* else on the dresser. *Only* the goldfish bowl. You'll see. *I promise! Okay? Okay, Mummy? Can I have a goldfish? Can I?*"

I am softening and Sheindl knows it. Rationalizations for my apparent capitulation run through my head. They range from "It may do good for my Sheindl to be more in tune with nature than I was—why should she inherit my neuroses?" (She certainly has enough of her own) to "Being responsible for the welfare of a fish could turn out to be a positive experience." The question is, for whom?

"So who will clean the bowl, feed the fish, and

change the water?" I demand. Sheindl isn't about to be defeated after she has come this far.

"I will, Mummy, Of course!" Sheindl says with wide-eyed ingenuity. "I simply can't *wait* to do it."

And that's how it comes to pass that a triumphant Sheindl arrives home with a fish in a clear plastic bag, a bowl and a container of fish food.

"The fish must be fed four flakes a day," she says knowingly, as if she had trained for a career in raising goldfish. The house has that festive air that is generally reserved for bringing home a new baby. A fish in the family! Sheindl fills the bowl, before her admiring siblings, a father trying to hide his smirk of amusement, (he was partly responsible for this situation, because when she asked him for the fish, he said "ask your mother") and a queasy mother.

When she sees the fish bowl full of water, Sheindl realizes that as caregiver it is her duty to introduce the fish to its new home. That is when she wavers. Dumping a squirmy, slimy fish into the bowl suddenly does not seem quite so appealing.

"Know what?" Sheindl announces, looking at six-year-old Avrumi. "I am even going to let you empty the fish into the water," she says graciously. Sheindl holds out the bag, trying to refrain from gagging.

The first fish feeding that night is a celebration. Sheindl takes a deep breath and drops one flake into the bowl, standing at a reasonable distance lest the fish launch a surprise attack. The fish surfaces and snaps up the food.

Sheindl is in and out of bed quite a bit that night. Like a post partum mother, she keeps on checking to see if her charge is still alive through the night.

"Ugh! Mummy!" She calls loudly, as soon as she wakes up the next morning. I come running. "What's that?" She points to the fish, from whose tailfin a thread-like substance is dangling."

"Well, um, as you know, Sheindl, a fish is a living thing. And whatever it has to do, it will do...right in the fish bowl," I tell her as delicately as I can.

By now, Sheindl's original euphoria has noticeably dissipated, and her attitude ranges from concern for the fish's welfare, to disgust at its presence. The fish remains Sheindl's responsibility, but that does not keep her from delegating fish-related chores to her younger siblings.

"I don't understand. Where is your sense of responsibility (achrayus)? Isn't it a boy's job to clean out the fish bowl? Huh?" she turns to her brothers Avrumi and Binyamin, who are deeply engrossed in a game of Battleship.

Avrumi looks at her skeptically. "Ugh!" he replies before returning to the game.

Sheindl changes her tone. "Isn't the fish cute," she

wheedles. "Poor thing. All it needs is some fresh water. You know what? I'll help you and bring the pail. You can empty the fish bowl into it and leave the fish there while you wash the bowl."

"Ugh!" This is from Binyamin.

Sheindl has to resort to Plan B. "Who wants my miniature calculator and organizer?" Sheindl asks casually addressing herself to the ceiling.

"Me!" Avrumi and Binyamin cry in unison.

"Well it's yours when you clean the fish bowl."

Faster than lightning Binyamin comes running with Sheindl's morning ablutions (*negel vasser*) pail.

"No!" shrieks Sheindl. "Ugh! Don't you dare! Take *your* pail." She pulls the pail from Binyamin, spilling its contents, soaking the two of them and the floor in the process.

Binyamin takes another pail, while Avrumi dips my flour sifter into the bowl to fish out the goldfish.

"**Not my sifter!**" I shriek—too late. The fish is floundering in the sifter. From this moment, my sifter takes on a newly created kosher category of "fish-ig" (to be used exclusively for the fish).

"Excuse me, but I've got homework to do," Sheindl calls over her shoulder as she flees the scene. I too have something very important to do just then and I leave for the porch to remember precisely what it is. We both return when Avrumi tells us that everything is back in order. Sheindl only enters the bathroom when the last sign of the fish and any residue is cleared up. Anything that had contact with the goldfish, or any fish for that matter, as far as she is concerned, is officially "ughy" now.

Please understand: Sheindl is by nature a very caring person. In her mind, a fish is no different than a human being. It is only in its outer appearance that it differs. A fishbowl existence must be miserable by any standard, Sheindl concludes. She buys some colorful stones and other décor for the fishbowl to brighten the fish's life. Unlike Sheindl, the fish seems comfortable in its new environment. The minute Sheindl snaps her finger above the bowl it surfaces and opens its mouth.

Sheindl carries the fish's welfare like personal baggage. She worries that the fish is lonely, therefore spends time sitting near the bowl to keep it company, lest it die of loneliness. To ease her load, Sheindl buys another goldfish, hoping it will take care of its emotional and social needs. Her attitude to the fish is a unique combination of concern, empathy and revulsion.

Every second day, Avrumi and Binyamin clean the mess two goldfish make in the fishbowl. The whole operation takes longer than before because of all the stones, shells and *tchotchkes* that needed rinsing.

Sheindl has stopped offering bribes for their help. The boys, now fishbowl-cleaning veterans, forget that it was originally Sheindl's job

"Nu! How can you let the fish swim in such a dirty bowl?" Sheindl stands over her brothers like a taskmaster. "Nu?! Do your job!"

At first, the goldfish swim around the bowl, apparently in playful circles. After a few days Sheindl, an expert by now, notices that goldfish #1 is aggressively pushing the newcomer to one side, while at other times it chases it and snaps at its tail. What is even more troubling is when Sheindl raises her hand over the bowl to feed the fish, fish #1 nudges "newcomer" aside and eats its portion. The poor newcomer can only eat what fish #1 leaves over, which is usually nothing.

Watching the bullying without being able to stop it (threats of expulsion do not seem to scare Fish #1) takes a heavy toll on Sheindl's emotions. Fish #1 becomes progressively fatter and stronger, while the new one become slower and weaker. It takes two weeks to realize that the smaller fish is in mortal danger. The fishy dream is turning into a nightmare.

One Sabbath the little fish barely swims. It floats listlessly not even attempting to reach for its food. I notice that Sheindl too has lost her appetite. In fact, she looks downright listless, too. She leaves for her friend's home soon after the Sabbath meal.

We all avoid the fishbowl. When the men come home from synagogue after sundown (*Motsei Shabbos*) Sheindl asks her father to check on the fish. The scene that awaits him is all too sad. The emaciated fish floats lifelessly on its back, while fish #1 swims triumphantly like an Olympic champion around the bowl. Without a usurper, Fish #1 reclaims rightful ownership of his fishbowl turf once again. From that day, Sheindl avoids the fishbowl. A clearly egomaniacal fish is not one she cares to befriend. My vague explanation about the Law of the Fishbowl is in vain.

Once again, Avrumi and Binyamin come to the rescue. They empty the dead fish into the toilet bowl. For the next few years, Sheindl spends minimum time in the bathroom.

Katie, my cleaning lady, is never so warmly welcomed as she is when she comes the following Thursday. We offer her Fish # 1 to add to the rest of the gang in her large, fancy tank, hoping it will learn humility now that **it** would be the newcomer.

Sheindl gradually begins to smile again, and in a short while progresses to wishing, wanting and finally needing again. Soon enough she is desperate once more. There is only one thing that can make her happy. Shoshya had just gotten a piano, and has enlightened Sheindl about the eternal delights of music that could be achieved by owning a piano of that caliber.

"It must be nice to have a piano," Sheindl muses, her arm resting on the windowsill as I fold the laundry. I know better than to tamper with pure, unsullied desire. Why destroy a perfectly good longing by fulfilling it? I immediately change the subject.

Grit Your Teeth—and Smile

Whoever coined the expression "million dollar smile," must know all about orthodontists. I know of families who have invested so much in their children's teeth that their cumulative debt equals the United States Gross National Product. For the parents it is the "million dollar cry."

Orthodonty is a relatively new industry whose success is fuelled by horror stories about the terrible consequences suffered by people who do not have their teeth improved. Orthodontists have estimated that about ninety-nine out of every hundred children are born with a dental impediment. Withholding treatment will have catastrophic consequences, possibilities range from developing a limp and psychological trauma, to chronic pneumonia. The remaining one percent, feeling deprived of a social rite, have their teeth enhanced, so as not to stand out in a crowd.

The first visit to the orthodontist is the decisive one. After that it becomes a lifetime partnership. Every few weeks there will be updates and appointments that will continue for the rest of your days. Consent to fitting your child with braces, and postpone the marriage of your oldest child for another five years, until the teeth are perfectly aligned. By the time all the teeth are straightened out, you will have advanced to the next stage of treatment—consulting plastic surgeons to eliminate your wrinkles.

A whole generation is under construction. Their open mouths resemble the steel beams of the foundations of an apartment complex. Hard as it is to understand children under normal circumstances, with a mouth full of strings and elastics, retainers and headgear, one must keep a ten-foot distance to avoid the spray and splutter that comes with every word. Their tongues constantly battle with the metallic gear that fences them in.

Had my grandparents ever visited an orthodontist's office they would have jumped out the window and fled. One glance at the wires and screws would have been enough to trigger their fears of torture chambers. As a twenty-first-century mother, my experience tells me that their assumptions are not so far from the truth.

The children, their mouths cluttered with metal and plastic, struggle with their lunches and with their conversation. With night gear and head gear they look like aliens.

Orthodonty has joined forces with the fashion industry, and it is saturated with gimmicks that entice the children to whine and beg their parents to allow them the *privilege* of braces. New innovations pop up, and the choices are limitless. There are colourful rubber bands that snap the jaws back together whenever the mouth is opened. With scented retainers; no matter what one eats, the breath suggests a recently devoured bouquet of lilacs or strawberries. Glow-in-the-dark retainers do have some practical value, like the girl in the forest, who, thanks to her shiny retainer, was found by the searchers when she opened her mouth to yawn.

Orthodonty is still in its pioneering stages. They have yet to come out with braces that have a matching metal brush that plays your favorite song, using the teeth as keynotes while manoeuvring the brush into the crevices between tooth and wires. How about battery operated braces or retainers to massage the gums and bleep whenever there is some food stuck somewhere? The teachers' union might have an interesting response to such a proposition. Who can handle a class of beeping and buzzing mouths?

The initial visit to an orthodontist will catapult you

to an entirely new lifestyle. Ask my best friend Shoshana! In the past she managed to raise eight children very well, but three retainers later, her life is in shambles. Shoshana spends approximately thirty-two hours per month just looking for lost retainers. Sit near her at social events, and her orthodonty stories will keep you so enthralled that when the lights go out you won't even be aware that the hall has emptied.

Even as I write this, I am trying to untangle my son's side-curl (*peyos*) from the retainer that is connected to it with silly putty. How it got there is a long story, but it does not beat the one where two retainers were mistakenly exchanged at the school lunch table.

The biggest problem with orthodontists is that they change procedures and equipment faster than they change the clippings on the wall. We end up sitting in an orthodontist's office more frequently than we visit a mother-in-law, and wait while staring at a fish bowl (if we are lucky) and posters of rotten teeth or fangs (representing the alternative to braces) or at that glorious million-dollar-smile to which we all aspire.

I rarely show my teeth these days, but as soon as the last child has completed the orthodontic ritual, and I have paid the last bill (if I still have my teeth), just watch me smile.

Good Health Hazards

Healthy living is a healthy industry for those who promote herbs, balms and therapies of all kinds. New theories discount those that are in vogue, followed by new innovations that become encoded in the statutes of health care, until the next theory germinates (excuse the pun), and voids those that were previously held to be sacred. Thus the more new information that circulates about health care or alternate health, the more confusion and mental anguish. This subsidizes the fields of psychology and mental health.

"Whatever is the matter?" I ask Chedva; when I meet her on the city bus sighing and mopping her brow. "Are you feeling alright?"

"No, not really," she answers while adjusting her bulging pocketbook which is poking into her grumpy neighbour. "I was perfectly fine an hour ago until I went to the health food store for some honey to bake cookies. I browsed through the pamphlets and book section. Those health book titles yelled out to me 'You're dead, unless you shape up by eating....or by...' I am utterly confused. Since I stepped out of that store I feel my blood pressure rising. I wonder if the damage from the years of coffee and cake are reversible. I must find some time and space to clear my head with yoga and meditation. I only scanned three pages of the book *Fit for Life*, and... and...I see I am not fit for it."

Her chin droops onto her chest and her eyes are moist with angst.

"Don't get so worked up," I comfort her. "I just saw the name of a young naturopathic doctor in the obituaries. It says he died a natural death. He wrote a bestseller about the virtues of that Gin thing, or Ginseng...or whatever. He laughed all the way to the bank while chewing on it—and he choked."

"So now you are going to comfort me with someone else's misfortune?" snaps Chedva. "There is no other way. I must turn my life around and acquire good health habits." She expresses such determination that I ruminate over her outburst after she alights at the next stop.

Since that meeting, Chedva is my health guru. She invests in every new health book on the market, crowding out the religious books that line the bookshelves. Keeping fit comes with its own code of laws (*halochos*)! Her language too is more sophisticated. Her sentences are interspersed with fewer exclamations of "Oy vey!" She replaces that with a more chic vocabulary rich with words ending with "pathy" or "path", such as "naturopath," or "homeopath, psychochopath..." and other words that relate to her newly-beaten path ostensibly leading to good health.

Her list of different therapies is longer than the list of diseases. I discover that so much of what we do every day is called a therapy—for example goofing off can also be relaxation "therapy." Humor therapy, light therapy, art therapy. I am contemplating introducing the game of checkers as a full-fledged field of checkerpathy. This would help the self worth of people who think they're wasting precious time. They could transform this preoccupation into a career.

Chedva's latest recommendation is aromatherapy.

"Oh, that!" I tell her. "I settle household odours with Lysol and Mr. Clean."

"Oh, no!" she reprimands me patronizingly. "That is poison! Aromatherapy is not for cleaning the house, but for one's physical and mental health. You inhale the scent of the healthiest herbs. I have a powder that contains the essential oils from seaweed and all kinds of exotic flowers and herbs. I empty it into the bathtub where I relax and inhale. It is good for arthritis, cures asthma, makes you younger, enhances family relation-ships, cures eczema and gout, prevents the flu, makes your mother-in-law more reasonable, and improves your complexion. I started using it this morning, and already I see a difference."

"So do I." I interrupt, "But why does your skin look like a coloring book?"

Chedva goes to the mirror to check what I am talking about, and shrieks. She rummages through the garbage to check the powder and discovers that she has bathed in a package of crayon sharpening that her daughter Basya has prepared for her arts and crafts assignment.

"So what did you smell when you inhaled? I asked

"The crayons were the fruity-smelling ones," she answers quite abashed. This episode affects her health in an unanticipated direction.

Chedva invests her energies into an organic vege-table garden that is the pride of the neighborhood. In her back yard she sports a compost heap higher than a skyscraper. Her family is not so enthusiastic about her new preoccupation.

"My friends get medicine only when they are sick. Why do I need it if I am well?" complains her son Tovy as he gags on a spoonful of flax seed oil blended with non-pasteurised honey and ground almonds.

Then comes the garlic period.

"Excellent against pinworms, earaches, viruses or bacteria!"

Strings of hanging garlic curtain her kitchen window. Not only do the pinworms disappear, but also any living creature within the radius of a mile. No wonder garlic is called a miracle herb. Perhaps one day it will be put to good use in warfare—healthy warfare sure beats bombs.

Chedva loses weight and strength under the strain of convincing her family to share her new lifestyle. In a moment of weakness she makes a wry joke that she is getting sick of getting healthy.

"I know just what you need." I offer her a plan. "Come over to my house. I have a "good-old-days" therapy for you."

We sit down to a table set with coffee and cheesecake, bagels, lox and blintzes. We indulge, and giggle as we look through our old yearbooks.

"Thanks for the great time," says Chedva before leaving, looking radiant and relaxed. "Though the food is not exactly what I had in mind...."

Shrugging my shoulders, I answered nonchalantly. "It is not so bad Chedva. After all this is what we grew up with—it's so *natural*."

In the Ways of our Fathers

The month preceding the New Year (Rosh Hashona) is Elul, a time when G-d is receptive to those who sincerely wish to mend their ways through repentance, prayer and charitable deeds. Repentance (*Teshuva*) involves soul-searching, admitting our errors and resolving not to repeat them, and changing our behavior. The special mood of Elul leads us to the day we ask G-d to forgive us our past sins for no other reason than his overwhelming mercy.

The momentum for self-improvement intensifies around me. Facing our failings is a humbling experience. Priorities are evaluated as inspirational tapes sprout like mushrooms after rain. Hearts and ears tune in to lofty words that help us aspire to spiritual goals. History has a rich pool of spiritual leaders (*tsaddikim* —people of high spiritual integrity, who are not necessarily but often are leaders) to emulate in this quest. The vibrant images of spiritual giants as heard through stories since childhood, motivate us to aspire to their levels.

I am overcome with zeal at the thought of the approaching New Year, and the impending Day of Atonement. I wish to reincarnate into the spiritual hero of every story I ever heard, within an hour. My expectations of myself are brutal. I do my repentance (*teshuva*) with energy, until I proudly feel that I have pushed my head through the clouds almost reaching the Heavenly Throne. It does not take much to remind me that I have barely reached the first step, as I belly flop back in the direction of earth with a thud. Spiritual improvement does not come so easy.

For a while, I think I am heading in the right direction, when I try to introduce the spirit of Reb Nachum Ish Gam Zu into my house. Reb Nachum was a spiritual giant. Over two thousand years ago he was approached by the Jews to intervene on their behalf in times of trouble. When there was no rain for a long period, he interceded from heaven for rain and immediately the earth was soaked. His faith was absolute, and he believed that every act of G-d, even if it is painful, is for our benefit. "This also is for benefit!" (*Gam zu letoivo!*) was his trademark response. That is how he became known as Reb Nachum, the man who believed that "this also ..." (*Ish Gam Zu*).

I try to adopt his attitude and thus strengthen my faith and pass on this quality to the family. A broken dish, a dysfunctional washing machine, an order that arrives late—always elicits an exclamation of *gam zu letoivo!* I repeat this mantra feeling very uplifted.

My first real test comes one morning after Raizy is downstairs on schedule waiting for her school bus. About eight seconds after I hear the bus motor fade away, I turn around and am surprised to see that self-same Raizy that I had personally dispatched downstairs, sniffling behind me.

"I just ran up for a tissue," she says with the air of one for whom time stands still.

After my initial shriek, I swallow some air, and remember to show enough restraint and exclaim "*Gam zu letoivo!*"—albeit a few tones louder than the holy Reb Nochum Ish Gam Zu said it.

"*Gam zu letoivo!*" I repeat, handing her the tissues, then under the same breath, "*How many times do I have to tell you not to come upstairs when the bus is coming?* Well ... *gam zu letoivo.* So now I have my program for today all set out for me. How am I going to get you to school? I have to be at the dentist in fifteen minutes. Oh well . . . *gam zu letoivo.*"

After repeating that virtuous statement at least thirty times before Raizy is safely deposited in school, she understands the words are Morse code equivalent for "Look what a troublemaker you are to ruin your mother's day. I could scream!"

The famous words were the hallmark of the holy

Reb Nachum Ish Gam Zu, but they fail to elevate me. I am still the frazzled mom who cannot control her anger, which means that I do not sincerely believe that there is a higher purpose to the things that happen in our lives. If things happen differently than I had planned I should be accepting and glad that there is One who knows better what is good for me. To truly improve myself, I must first try more elementary techniques.

I try a different tactic. I will emulate Reb Shammai, a leader from the generation of the Tanaim, who were the spiritual and intellectual greats who furiously debated in the houses of study in their mission to compile the Talmud. The debates were divided between the disciples of the house of Shammai and the house of Hillel. Shammai always took a stricter stance in his interpretations in the code of Jewish Law. He focused on a more literal interpretation of the text of the bible, whereas Hillel, who was a descendant of King David, took a more lenient stance. Shammais was not tolerant of spiritual weakness.

Emulating Shammai barely lasts one day. I go about the house with the attitude of a reformed smoker, oblivious to the inability of my family to keep up with my noble standards. Throughout my Shammai performance they keep their distance. I accept no behavior that has no heavenly intent, and heaven help anyone who stands in my way. My virtuosity culminates in a long prayer (*tefillo*) and a fit of tears, after which I realize that I am being Shammai, but for the grace of Shammai. It does not take me long to switch to the tactics of the compassionate Hillel.

Reb Hillel was a sage who was famous, among other things, for love of his fellow man. His patience was legendary. A bet was made between two simple people, that one would give the other 400 zuzzim (the currency of the day) if he could enrage Reb Hillel. The man chose a time close before the Sabbath when Hillel was engrossed in preparations, to come and annoy him with ridiculous questions. Hillel responded with empathy and interminable patience until the person cursed him for making him lose the bet.

I use Reb Hillel as my guide. My cup overfloweth with patience. I tolerate tantrums and devote unlimited time on anyone who demands it. I do relaxation breathing exercises as I attempt to enforce bedtime. My gentle sigh does not go unnoticed, and for some reason it is intimidating to those dearest to me. I clear up the debris of scattered toys with a smile, rather than impose force. To accentuate my heroism and righteousness I sigh while getting the family together at the supper table, which is something like trying to assemble a prayer quorum (*minyan*) in Timbuktu. I sigh silently and I sigh gently and sometimes for emphasis a little louder, until I sound like someone who suffers from emphysema.

I become so docile and relaxed that eventually the house takes on the atmosphere of a carnival, and I am forced to put aside the ways of our fathers and revert to being an earthly policeman to restore law and order.

Joseph, whose nature is consistent and dependable, takes my repentance "du jour" in stride, curious about which mood his volatile wife will greet him with on the other side of the door. I give him plenty of exercise for self-improvement. Being patient with my various approaches that change by the hour is challenging— and that is an understatement.

I pay much lip service to the beloved Reb Zushe, a disciple of the Baal Shem Tov, the founder of the Hassidic movement who inspired followers hundreds of years ago. He spread joy wherever he went, and his joy was not dependent on materialism. He never worried about materialistic and mundane things like food on the table or clothing, though he often was hungry. I react harshly to complaints from any family member, such as "I have nothing to wear!" or "I don't like spinach!" or "Shloimo is deliberately holding up the bathroom by taking so long to brush his teeth!"

I shun materialism with a passion.... that is, until I check the closets and conclude that the children have nothing to wear for the upcoming holy days (*Yom Tov*). Then I shop till I drop, or till the money runs out, (whichever comes first). I vacillate for over twenty minutes over whether the shoe or shirt is nice enough for the Sabbath (*shabbosdig*) or not.

Like Zushe, I do not worry on *Yom Tov* about having food on the table, because unlike Reb Zushe, my freezer is packed with enough to supply an army. I prepared it long before I stopped being materialistic.

There are no shortcuts to being a better person. Spiritual elevation cannot be attained in a crash course from Elul until after the Holidays (*yomim tovim*). It takes a lifetime to reach one's potential (if it can ever be reached). Emulating the actions of great people is not enough. It needs a thorough cleansing of the heart and mind to achieve their status.

I must work from the inside with a humble spirit and a desire to grow. I must face each test moment-by-moment and situation-by-situation. I know that up there, it is not the perfection that counts as much as the direction. Please G-d when I pray to You, I know my merits are lacking. I also know that You are generous in your evaluations. You understand I am human and balancing this world with the next is a challenge. You understand, and seek to justify. I can count on You to at least give me some credit for trying.

Weather Related

Winter is a unifying experience. It arouses com-passion and a mutual understanding that only the cold weather, or being victimized by terror, can bring about. We make up for the falling temperature by producing inner warmth, as we become one big family of fellow sufferers, all fighting the same enemy, the cold.

I normally never exchange more than a "Good Sabbath" (*Gut Shabbos*) or a shake of the head when I meet with Mrs. Guttskep during the year. However, when we bump into each other in the deep frost of the winter, with my collar over my ears, and my shoulders hunched forward to get the maximum warmth out of my coat, she becomes my mother.

"So cold! Where are your gloves, deary?" She admonishes me.

The below zero temperatures have made us Canadians a friendlier society, and a more physically fit society. After shoveling snow, our main athletic pastime becomes pushing cars with revved up engines and spinning wheels out of snow banks. Prrrrrr Prrrrrr!

These winter sounds replace the chattering and chirping birds of the summer.

Otherwise, there is silence. The frost absorbs sounds. Outside one cannot even talk. Words freeze in mid air. Communication is by smoke signals emitted through red noses. For all one knows, those muffled shapes wrapped from head to toe could just as well be portable chimneys. Winter is not a time to look pretty. There are no people loitering on street corners, or mothers exchanging homeopathic remedies, or men standing in front of the bank, fingering their car keys as they discuss what they would do if they were prime minister. It is self evident that even he/she would also run indoors. We are all in a mad race to reach our destination before frostbite beats us to it.

When the scientists threaten and warn us to change our lifestyles to avoid global warming, we Canadians dismiss them and advise them to address their concerns to the nomads in the Sahara desert. For us, global warming is a blessing. There would not be such a thing as Mad Cow disease, because the cows would not go mad from standing in a freezing barn for six months of the year. With global warming we would not have to sit inside and overload the electrical circuits, or pour gallons of oil into our furnaces, to warm our houses. People prefer sitting on a warm balcony, any day.

Cold weather is brutal. It is not much fun waiting outdoors for the slow-moving frozen school buses while the limbs become stiff and tears freeze to the little faces. The buses arrive home late, because the bus monitors must spend time unwrapping, and then rewrapping each child to ensure that the right child is sent to the right house.

I try very hard to find other positive aspects to winter, besides thinking it could be worse. I comfort myself with the worse possibility of living in Iraq—a tad too hot! It takes a small walk outside to realize that the cold is a great socializer. People who find communicating difficult for lack of something to talk about, have a custom-made topic. It is socially acceptable to be repetitious. Best of all it gives us something to brag about to the Americans, who are used to setting records.

"Yes my child. What do you know about the cold? Come to Montreal, and THEN we'll talk about the cold!"

Canada is a relatively peaceful country. This can be attributed to our winters. The cold weather may be a very dull topic, but it is not controversial. When people talk about the weather, they do not fight. Even leaders of powerful countries know this, and they travel around using the weather in their dialogue with world leaders to avert war.

The world would be a much safer if all they had to talk about were the cold. For example if the British Prime Minister had an audience with the Premier of China, it would go something like this:

"Mr. Premier, we have very fine Shetland wool garments in England which would really keep your nationals warm in the winter. We are ready to sell at an excellent price if you make it mandatory for every Chinese citizen to own one. You will see how much warmer the people will be and how much more productive."

"Well, Mr. P.M. that means about three billion people"

"Uh-oh, I am not sure we have enough sheep. You know what, let us exclude Hong Kong."

Of course the Chinese Premier would use this occasion to his political gain. "We would subsidize a scarf for everyone in Tibet, but then you must agree that Tibet is considered part of China. And by the way, we'll knit them ourselves. It's cheaper that way." When the subject turns controversial, the prime minister could change the subject by rubbing his fingers and saying "Whew it's cold!"

It is very difficult to consistently stick to the subject of cold, in places like the Middle East, but the cold can be a productive springboard to other topics of conversation.

"Hello, what do you say to the weather? It's cold, no?" ..."Are you cold?"... "We are so-o cold." "My heater is working over time... You have gas heating..." "I have electricity..." " Too cold to go to school. Is there school tomorrow, it's cold?" "He has the flu." "It's because of the cold..." "Wear gloves, it's cold..." "I am making warm soup for supper—it's so cold..." "The skiing industry is losing money, because it is too cold..." "I am going to Florida because of the cold..." "A fur coat is just what I need in this cold." Cold! Cold! Cold! "Achoo!"

The four letter word "cold" is repeated more often in the space of winter than words like "okay," or "and" or "the." The bus stop is a perfect spot for weather related communication. A crowd of people stand around shifting feet, hands in pockets, shoulders slouched, shielding themselves against the wind. At regular intervals an anxious passenger will step over to the curb, crane his neck to catch a glimpse of the bus. The rest of the passengers surge forth expectantly like hungry lions in the zoo at feeding time. Just behind you in the line, is a disgruntled woman with icicles hanging from her hat, and you get the feeling that she is dangerously determined to push herself on the coming bus before you.

"Cold, huh?" is the obvious thing to say. Her answer

is optional. Tensions immediately ease. You suddenly become fellow sufferers rather than antagonists.

"Freeeeezing!" she answers and wraps the scarf more tightly over her mouth to emphasise the point, and you know she has relaxed and the danger is over. Instead of picking on each other, the weather becomes the punching bag.

"Unbelievably cold," you say, as you dig deeper into your pockets to make sure the bus ticket is there.

"Some winter!"

"Awesome, eh?"

That is about as intellectual as your conversation will get, especially with the mouth and ears covered by scarves and earmuffs. It is socially acceptable to repeat the "conversation" with anyone who growls in your direction.

For someone with a little more imagination using weather as an opening topic could initiate a broader conversation such as health or politics, but these conversations will conclude only once you are on the warm bus.

"Ouch, the cold really is hard on the bones."

"Arthritis? My doctor tells me I should go to Arizona."

"Really? Who is your doctor?"

"Dr. Donald Duck. He is chief of entocopology, or something like that, and..."

If the banter carries on long enough it could conclude with a final decision to go ahead with the renovation job that has been in planning for the last five years.

'My daughter insisted I go to this doctor for my frequent headaches."

"Headaches? I suffered for four years until I was told that it was from mould in the basement?"

"Really? Who did you use for your renovations...?"

Her frozen fingers will shiver as she writes down the name in letters that are as jagged as icebergs.

For all we know, the beautiful homes that we pass by daily were inspired by a chat in the cold winter weather.

The dialogue on the streets however is friendlier than at home. In spring, a warm welcome awaits anyone who steps in the house, and greetings are exchanged at the door. In winter, anyone stepping in the front door is greeted by a united chorus of hidden voices emanating from every corner of the house.

"Who opened the door?"

"Are we living in tents around here?"

"It's freezing!"

"Close the door!"

Though winter may not be the most convenient of seasons, at least we can observe it in a cotton shirt from the confines of a warm home in Canada and not in the

Russian Gulag. I comfort myself that while the icicles form and the mountains of snow make boundaries between the sidewalk and the street, there is something splendid going on. Spring is on its way. Under the ice the trees are going through the initial stages of revival. Fruits, grains and vegetables, after a seasons rest, are being blessed to burst forth once more to provide us with continued nourishment. Why feel handicapped, when we know this is part of the ritual that leads us into spring? We are all part of that plan, and we should celebrate and relate to one another like one big family.

So fellow brothers and sisters, much as I feel the bond between all of us, please excuse me while I enjoy these heart-warming thoughts as I defrost while hibernating under a heavy blanket. It's freezing outside! Wake me up after winter.

Memories, Memorials
and Shavuot

Every night another day in the counting of the forty-day interval (*omer*) between Passover (*Pesach*) and the harvest festival (*Shavuot)* is ticked off the calendar. Under most circumstances Shavuot is a festival of joy for many reasons, one of them being that the Torah was handed down on Mount Sinai.

However, the weeks leading to the arrival of *Shavuot* evokes bittersweet emotions—joy and sadness, particularly among the Jews of Hungarian descent. It was around this time of the year during the Second World War that whole cities of Jews who had been rounded up and forced into ghettos, were transported en masse in cattle cars to their death in Auschwitz and other concentration camps, or shot on the outskirts of the forests. Families were torn apart, and dragged to their death.

After the war the straggling remainder left Europe for more receptive shores.

The survivors from these old European neighborhoods joined together as one extended family to form their own synagogues (*shuls*). Since they had no confirmation of the dates of the death of their families, they adopted as mass memorial days, the days leading to Shavuot which were the last recorded dates that their loved ones were seen alive, when their cities and towns were made *Judenrein* or "cleared of Jews," and when the trains arrived in Auschwitz. It is on these days when each survivor recites the mourning prayer (*Kaddish*) to sanctify the souls of the martyrs.

The spirits of the souls who died in the Holocaust take over the atmosphere of the synagogue. The few prayer quorums of ten men (*minyonim*) led by the dwindling elderly survivors, many widowed and frail by now, are never too far from their Book of Psalms and their study books; they study and pray in memory of the souls of their lost families. They repeat the names of parents, children, siblings, and friends who left no descendents to recite the mourning prayer on their behalf.

As the days close in on Shavuot, after the morning service more members of the synagogue spread out onto the tables their offerings of sponge cakes and spirits. The blessings said over them by the congregation will be a spiritual elevation for the souls. *"Lechaim! Lechaim!"* (To Life!) Good wishes are exchanged between one another for the departed and for the living. The congregation divides into quorums of ten (*minyonim*) so each survivor has the opportunity to lead the mourning prayers (*Kaddish*). These men have weathered difficult times. They are the almost annihilated link of the chain leading back to the receiving of the Torah.

Mr. S, a regular, prays every day, and he often leads the prayers for the congregation. His prayers can hardly be heard through his sobs. He was once forcibly assigned to the crew of hapless Auschwitz inmates whose job it was to shovel the bodies from the gassings into blazing fires. This was a short-term job, for at regular intervals these teams were inevitably murdered to destroy all evidence of the atrocities. He was fourteen when he was left for dead after a mass shooting. He crawled out from under a pile of bodies that were about to be shoveled into the inferno, and through a succession of miracles made his escape. He made a deal with his Maker. "Help me live. Let me serve you for the rest of my life with heart and soul."

He escaped and lived like a hunted animal in the forests. He survived the war, and discovered that he had been destined to be the only survivor from all his immediate family. There was no one but him to avenge

their souls. He does this the way he knows best—by perpetuating their faith and carrying on their legacy with the memories that they left him. He has carried this responsibility for more than sixty years.

Fire fuels his prayers, and he lives with gratitude every moment of his life. Though his beard is white and he is slightly bent, he is oblivious to the attention he draws in whichever synagogue he prays. Morning prayers (*shacharis*), sundown prayers (*mincha*), or evening prayers (*maariv*), he sways like a branch in a storm, clapping his hands and raising his voice above all the congregants.

The spirits of the families and whole communities that were turned into smoldering embers mingle there together with children and grandchildren of the survivors, to celebrate the holiday that began four thousand years ago. They mourn over what could have been their extinction.

In the beginning a system of priority for who would lead the prayers in the synagogue was established by winding a rope around a hand and elbow. Each member would take hold of a section of the rope. When the rope was unwound the ones closest to the ends took precedence in leading the quorum.

Three generations later the number of survivors has dwindled. They no longer need to grip a spot on a rope for this privilege.

In the years following the Holocaust, congregations like this were mostly survivors and strangers to this part of the world. They struggled to return to the only way of life that they knew, the normalcy they remembered before the upheaval. They were beginning to feel the luxury of dreaming of a future, and be parents to a new generation of children, to whom such stories as theirs belonged in Hassidic tales. They handed down the same ground rules that they were given, and saturated them with meaning.

The temptations of modern times extend their tentacles. The influence of the survivors has generated some immunity against embracing the new wave of attitudes that the world generally accepts as a valid lifestyle. This aged and bent generation is a living reminder that the attitudes and philosophies of mankind are frail at best or dangerous and destructive at worst. It was civilization's leaders who applied the noble concept of cleansing and purity to killing the sick, the elderly, the mentally incapacitated, and the sub-human races. This purification could have continued until only evil remained.

Though the new generation by far outnumbers the survivors, the flavor of Europe vibrates. The memorial days (*yahrzeiten*) are not only for their parents but for the legacy that their parents bequeathed, that dates back to the Spanish Inquisition, to Rome, to Babylonia, and even further back to Mount Sinai.

Thousands of years, and better and worse times come and go. The settings change in every generation but on the shelf, the flicker of the flames of the memorial candles remains. Attitudes and values change, and as they do we are predisposed to the ideas and whims of the day, like a candle flame that flares with full flame and then settles, bowing to the winds of time. History shows us that what is fashionable and proper in one era can be deemed cruel and immoral in another. The most stable foothold is, through good times and bad, to cling to the tried and true values handed down to us by our parents.

From Pogroms to Programs

Hanukkah is a story of repression, resistance, miracles and hope. In Judea in the second century before the Common Era (200 BCE), the Greco-Syrian King Antiochus forbade the Jews living under his rule to worship any but the Greek gods. This resulted in a rebellion and a war. After three years of struggle the Jewish Maccabees drove the Greco-Syrians out of Judea. The Temple in Jerusalem had been desecrated and when it was purified there remained only a one-day supply of purified oil to burn in the Temple's menorah. A new supply could not be processed for another week. Miraculously the oil lasted the full eight days until a fresh supply was available. Hanukkah celebrates this miracle with eight days of candle-lighting.

At last count this week, it was one thousand, three hundred and fifty one repetitions, and it is only Wednesday. From the moment she stretches in the morning until her eyes close at night, my little kindergarten girl sings it repeatedly. Even the baby has picked up bits and pieces of the upcoming Hanukkah program. When his older sister goes to school, he takes over. There is no way I can forget that Hanukkah is around the corner.

For over two decades, each child has annually entertained me, with basically the same Hanukkah songs. The identical hand motions are assembled in different sequences from year to year. The tunes may slightly vary, and the rhyme of each stanza every year in a different order, are something like *meidel* (young girl), *dreidel* (a Hanukkah spinning toy). Both *latkes* (pancakes) and *kneidel* (dumplings) are strategically fitted in if it goes well with the rhythm. To see it once is to see it all, yet it thrills me each time.

A miniature Antiochus wears her crown slightly askew and she scratches the irritating gold-sprayed cardboard hanging on her forehead. The cushion on her tummy peeps out from under the satiny robe. Antiochus beckons for the ever-faithful servant, (a role reserved always for the child who loses her tongue). The servants make their appearances and disappearances, doing Antiochus's bidding, ripping the crepe pantaloons in their eagerness to be the best

possible servants. Of course no program is complete without a dancing cheese latke, or spinning dreidel, and candles with flaming orange headbands.

It is a strange phenomenon, but the more I am deluged with Hanukkah programs, the more moved I am by each impromptu performance during breakfast and through suppertime. It takes restraint to keep my face straight as the little actress prances, bows and waves her hand while singing familiar words and assembling them in an order that as yet does not quite make sense. I watch her coordinate her motions. With the utmost concentration she must bring out thumb, pointer and middle finger, and incorporate it into the tune, singing "one, two, and three." I can foresee her on stage with the rest of the choir, who will be at least three stanzas ahead by the time her fingers are correctly positioned at the exact angle required by her teacher. My child is a stickler for details.

I have been inspired by cantors, rejoiced with Hassidic melodies, classical and wedding music, but nothing is more heart wrenching than a row of fresh faced blushing little *latkes, dreidels,* and those that play the roles of Chana and her seven sons.

They *almost* sing together, each on a different squeaky key, occasionally catching a yawn, or stopping as they catch the eye of their family in the audience. They look earnestly to their nervous teacher for their next cue; she has been up many nights working on a suitable program.

The music begins and the story unfolds. Hanukkah today—Bubby (grandmother), Mummy, family friends, *dreidels, latkes*—happy things that can be felt, touched, and therefore understood. Lights shine brightly with the promise of happiness. It is their version of Hanukkah, their innocent story.

They sing and twirl, captivating the audience of adults, many of who are ten times their age. As we watch the children tell the story, we feel the joy, the bitterness, the hope and the faith they inspire. The spine tingles. The innocent purity of the children chanting blends with the reality of a story that represents who we are, and it wracks the emotions.

Yehudis (Judith) the ancient heroine stands over Holofernes the tyrant. We are served a bittersweet concoction as we are overcome with the cuteness of the children versus the chilling truth of our history. The intricacies of the story make it all the more profound. I see a People, trembling before a bitter fate. Yehudis goes on her mission ready to sacrifice her life for her people. The sweeter the child, the more pain I feel... many children in fear, being comforted by their parents behind the walls of their city. Children? Oh yes.... these children are singing, not knowing exactly what. Deep down they know there is something important, or why is the family so wrapped around the Hanukkah flames?

The children know the story of Hanukkah through gastronomical delights like *latkes*, donuts, *blintzes* and a moment in the spotlight. They understand the sweet delicious part of it, and are confident that like every story, the story of Hanukkah has a happy ending. They do not quite grasp the middle. I am overcome with sadness that innocence is so fleeting.

Eight little candles strut the stage. As they sing, I notice a few bubbies (grandmothers) wipe their eyes. They have lived their version of the Hanukkah story in Europe not that long ago. Their story of how they salvaged their precious margarine and potatoes from their meager food rations, defying the dull throbbing of hunger, defying their oppressors with their polished boots and guns, defying their own weariness. After a full day of backbreaking and humiliating dawn to dusk labor, hours of forming rows and standing in one position during the meticulous head counts (*tzeilappell*), bereft of socks and warm clothes to ward off the bitter cold— they believed in miracles.

They returned to their bunkers, and from their sparsely-woven blankets, they made wicks from some threads to light up their margarine candles in their potato candelabra. The tiny flames were their symbol of defiance and the fuel of faith that warmed them.

The Hanukkah candles flickered over the gaunt faces of breathing skeletons and lit an inner fire. It was not in the realms of their imagination to dream that one day the pogroms and the persecutions would be celebrated by programs.

In front of these bubbies, the children sing today. They are the miracle of light that their grandmothers never dared to dream of. They sing the same songs their grandparents sang. They do not understand it yet, but as they sing the story of Hanukkah, they sing of themselves and their parents and great grandparents from generations back. May G-d grant that every child everywhere will sing songs inside their hearts.

Summing Up a Story

Last night I pulled a chair up to the dining room table, and showed my eight-year-old son how to multiply big numbers. If ever I will reflect on the great and momentous events in my life, I will count this as one of them.

So, what, you ask, is the big deal? I have made greater exertion over a countless number of times. What parent is not ready and willing to put aside time or money or even their life for a child?

What is so special about last night is that I had instant gratification. My efforts have helped release the heavy burden on Lipa's shoulders. His mumbled "Thank you!" was loaded with feelings of appreciation and relief.

There is a fundraiser tea party tonight, and I drag

my feet, debating about whether to go. After supper, Lipa follows me from the kitchen, and in a half whisper, in his most pathetic tone, asks, "Can I come home earlier tomorrow?"

He had unsuccessfully tried to convince his father the day before that he needed a day off. Knowing that I am made of more porous dough he tries his salesman technique on me.

"Mommy, can I come home at four o'clock tomorrow?"

He gives me about five reasons, which I discount one after another. I prod him until he finally shows me a paper with fifty multiplication sums, of which he had done three, (all with wrong answers). He has to hand in the rest the next day, and he has no inkling about how to do it.

"I can't do it!" Big tears roll down his cheek.

"You can't now, but I will show you how and then you will know how to do it," I argue.

"But I can't!" He keeps repeating, as if I were expecting him to demonstrate the theory of relativity.

It takes me twenty minutes to convince him to just give it a try.

"If you can learn the Talmud, and understand that, then you will understand this. The Talmud is even more difficult. I can not help you with that, but I can help you with the math."

I beg him. I insist. I lecture him never to give up, and always to continue trying. Then I emphasize, "It must be very hard for you, to sit through class not knowing your work." His face relaxes and he is ready to communicate more rationally.

"When you don't understand, don't be shy to ask. Remember what we just read this week in the *Ethics of our Fathers*, "*Veloi Habayshon lomed*" (The abashed cannot learn). If you are too proud to ask, you will fall behind, and it will be harder and harder to catch up. Smart people admit that they do not understand. They ask, and then they get answers."

His tears drip onto his shirt.

"But I can't, I can't" he wails.

"Can you imagine me crying because the food I cook is too salty, or because the bread did not rise?" I ask him. "If that is all I can do when that happens, then you would always be eating heavy bread and bad tasting food."

Lipa's tears turned to giggles as he picture his mother crying over her supper.

"When things go wrong, I ask why they went wrong. I ask people who know. You know what Lipa, let's give it a try together."

Lipa loosens his shoulders and finally gives me a chance. After four multiplications, he grasps the concept of multiplying large numbers, and carrying to the next unit and he is able to do the rest on his own. After doing ten calculations he knows it so well, that any mistakes he makes are from careless overconfidence.

That night, he goes to bed tranquil. Together we have lifted a mountain.

Every parent who has raised children can relate little stories like this, and hundreds of stories that are far more outstanding. That is exactly why I am so deeply affected by what happened. *I almost missed this story.* Who knows how many opportunities for stories like this I have missed in the past?

I could have been at that party, enjoying the salads and the entertainment, oblivious to the dread that Lipa was experiencing. It was my dallying that had kept me from being at the fundraiser. Had I left earlier, Lipa would not have asked me if he could come home earlier. It had obviously taken time and effort for him to muster enough courage to ask my permission. Lipa knows very well that not knowing his work is definitely not an acceptable excuse for being absent from school.

My child could have ended up having a miserable day at school, feeling inadequate, stupid, and fearful of the wrath of the teacher. He could have lost his confidence. He could have been frustrated and angry, and translated his emotions into bad behaviour. The source of his frustrations could have passed me by, and

I could have misjudged him and treated him inappropriately. Events could have escalated and the happy ending might have been a sad one.

It scares me to think how many such stories I may have missed, because of bad timing, extraordinary circumstances, bad judgement, misunderstanding, or simply by not paying attention to signals. Raising children is like a dance on eggshells, knowing how to listen to a child, to what is unsaid, as much as to his or her words. It is a balancing act between rigidity on issues, and seeing and feeling with the child's mind. It is an exercise in communication, knowing when to say "no" without intimidating, and a test requiring limitless patience.

It saddens me to think how many people never realize that a child's unattended minor problems or misunderstanding are triggers to more complex problems. This story reminds me how delicately parents must tread, and how fragile we are. This simple story tells me that simple stories are not as simple as they are perceived to be.

Color Coded Calendar

Tending to family, participating in extended family events while accommodating friends and personal needs like shopping and appointments into the lifestyle is a major challenge. My friend Rivka has developed some interesting ways of coping.

If archaeologists ever dig up Rivka Sputz's calendar a thousand years from now, they may identify it simply as colorful hieroglyphics. It will need plenty of imagination to believe that people in this day and age could fit so much action into their agenda.

Rivka's calendar is always a splash of color for the coming three months, and after that it is splotched for the following six. Red stars mark first cousin's weddings, red circles for bar mitzvahs. Blue stars are for friends or relatives of secondary importance. Purple is for weddings that she must attend out of pity for the wedding party, and yellow marks are for those that gave presents at her family's weddings and therefore require reciprocation. Beige asterisks accompany doctor and dentist appointments. Fundraiser or charity events she must attend because the sister of the organizer shared a bungalow one summer in the country and even once lent her an onion, are marked in black. The Sabbaths are usually reserved for visiting friends who just had babies or some other family celebrations, or to listen to one of the speakers scheduled for that week. The calendar is marked sparsely with dots that represent obligations to attend one of the seven blessed feasts (*sheva brachos*) that follow the wedding of a newly married couple.

The haircutting ceremonies (*upsheren*) of little nephews, or children of friends who turn three are pink squiggles on the page, green for aerobic classes or PTA, and a few gold diamonds are splattered here and there to accommodate a few minutes of conversation with her husband Yossel, whose schedule is equally hectic. Rivka has a box with sixty-four crayons hanging beside the calendar.

Due to the intensity of the timetable of weddings, engagements, bar mitzvahs, and family affairs and celebrations (*simchas*) the Sputz family has developed a time-saving system. Rivka has even learned to save words. Discussions are concluded even before they begin.

" Why can't..." her children whine.

"Because I said so," Rivka answers. "Now brush your teeth, and we'll talk later."

She sends the loudest noisemaker to his room to cool down, refusing to get involved in investigations about who tore up whose homework.... because someone ate someone's cookie ... because yesterday that someone deliberately slammed the door while someone else was listening to a tape ... while the car that will take Rivka to the next wedding is honking its horn outside.

The Sputzs have become so time efficient that when Rivka metamorphoses from Cinderella in her flour encrusted duster to the elegant wedding guest, on the other side of the dressing room door, Sorreleh who is struggling with her homework, asks her mother for a sentence with the word 'harried.' Rivka complies with a hairpin between her teeth, while clasping the pearls around her neck. Farewell instructions are doled out all the way down the steps.

"Take the challah out of the oven by 10.30 p.m., and no, you may not go to Rochel's house to do homework.

As she slams the front door shut, the window above opens up and a child calls.

"Do I divide or multiply to get the area of a square."

Rivka is in the car by now so she rolls down the window and yells loudly so as to be heard as the car gathers momentum.

"Multiply, darling. You should always multiply!

Pedestrians passing by turn their heads and try to figure out what this unexpected blessing is all about.

Rivka will make her rounds through two weddings, meet her husband at a third and spend precious time together driving to Monsey, New York to drop in and congratulate the Gevurts family who are celebrating their daughter's engagement.

By one a.m. the colored symbols lose their importance. The next day's schedule has a different hue. Rivka, takes her calendar one day at a time. Perhaps many generations into the future, when scholars study her calendar, they will conclude that once upon a time the day must have consisted of thirty-six hours.

A Milestone

My neighbor adjusts her daughter's schoolbag as they wait for her bus. She turns around to reprimand her barefoot toddler, coaxing him to go back inside. Across the street, young Mrs. Pollak rakes leaves off the sidewalk. How is it that the world can follow a daily routine, when my life is undergoing a major revolution? After decades of being attached to babies and home, scheduling my life around feeding and nap times, reading, teaching and entertaining toddlers, my eleventh child, Lipaleh is leaving me alone to fend for myself. He is going to school—and there is no baby left at home to cheer me up!

I shiver in the cool fall wind, waiting for the familiar hiss of the school bus as it stops, and enviously watch a young mother trying to organize her little brood and get them across the street. I have barely got the hang of dealing with a family of children, (it takes many years, if ever, to learn) and I am suddenly confronted with a new lifestyle. I never imagined that having a few hours of my own could be so lonesome and difficult.

We had worked Lipaleh up to this moment. Every night, as my husband helps Lipa into his pyjamas, they sit on the couch and discuss school, how it looks, how it feels, how he was also once a little boy who went to school and one day became a father (*Tatti*). After this indoctrination Lipaleh begins to sound like an old school veteran.

Though Lipa has never been away from Mommy, he speaks by now about his teachers as if they are regular acquaintances, he knows some of his friends with whom he will be together in school, and also which pants and shirt he will wear on his first day. His brothers and sisters egg on his excitement and tell him countless school stories and details of the daily routine, refurbishing their stories to make it more exciting by the minute. Our efforts pay off and Lipa anticipates this day with joy.

I catch him just a second before he runs off the sidewalk in his enthusiasm to greet the bus that will take him to his new world. At this moment school means the thrill of a real school bus ride, like the one that takes his siblings every day, as he watches them

leave with his nose pressed to the window. This is not the fantasy bus in which he has been travelling for the past year on the living room couch, steering it with a pot lid and improvising the sound of the motor with his incessant rrrmmm, rrrmms. School, for Lipaleh, is the promise of being big, like his brothers and sisters, joining them in their shared understanding of lunch boxes, rabbis, friends, fun, books and crayons.

I almost choke over the lump that develops in my throat, and I worry about how he will cope without a Mummy handy at his beck and call.

"Let go!" I whisper to myself. "Give him a chance to develop a life of his own."

He ascends the giant steps of the bus like a brave soldier on a mission. As the door closes behind him the expression on his face as he turns to me tells me that just this second he has discovered a new reality. School is separation! It means leaving home and fending for one's self. Lipaleh's eyes follow me with one last look before they well up with shiny tears. I wave idiotically, like a cheerleader at camp until the bus turns the corner, and with it disappears a phase that has been with me for more than half my life.

The quietness in the house roars savagely as I close the door behind me. "It will only be for a few hours," I comfort myself. "It is my time now. No one else around, just the unmade beds, laundry and breakfast dishes." I call my husband at work, and try to tell him with as much complacency as possible that Lipaleh is on his way, but my voice shakes and I sniff into the phone and ruin his day. We have an unspoken system of communication where the more emotional I become, the more level-headed my husband sounds. He becomes an advisory board, telling me what I already know, or don't want to know.

"Listen, every child has to go through this once. It does not help to mope. He will be fine..."

I have lived long enough with Joseph to understand that his speeches are a cover to deal with his own emotions. So we hang up.

With a matter-of-fact air I pick up the toys Lipa left scattered, and his little slippers. Even the porridge remains on his plate are stark reminders of his absence. It is a hard day for Lipa and I make sure that I too will not enjoy it. I try to control the tears, but remember that there is no one around to see me and ask if I have a booboo in my eyes, or if I just cut onions. I do not have to explain. I let the tears fall and I can sob loudly, and sound as foolish as ever.

The tears subside and I feel as if I had just undergone a cleansing, and I can think more rationally. One phase is over but new ones keep coming. Why cry when this is one of the moments I dreamed about? I should be laughing, stupid! I would much rather laugh than cry. I thank *G-d* for reaching this beautiful moment.

Three weeks later I wake up groggy and I selfishly look forward to sending Lipa off for the day and having some time to myself. I have just discovered that within the next seven or so months, I will have more to laugh (and cry) about. Once again, for the twelfth time, I will have little company with whom to share my day.

Telphonitis

After trying for four days to reach me, my bank manager suggests I install a kids' line at home. I am embarrassed to tell him that they have one already. What I really need is a telephone line for *me*. All of us are infected with the chronic disease of the times—we have a severe case of telephonitis. The major symptom of this disease is an inability to function for five minutes without a telephone pressed to our ear.

I need access to the phone. I stand breathing loudly near Chaya, who is talking a mile a minute. Somehow, her conversation loses impetus; girl talk is no fun with an audience staring you down. Her index finger goes up in the air, signalling to me "just one minute". With a purple face and steam coming out of my ears, my pursed lips silently shape the words: "May I have the phone?"

Again I am confronted with the waving finger in the air, and a look that is begging me for patience, pleading that I should not embarrass her. She is so tense, and does not even listen, or care what is being said at the other end of the line. She cannot interrupt her friend in the middle of a sentence that is as long as the United States Constitution!

"Wow!" a polite giggle to prove that she *is* listening (even though her mother is distracting her) and then a comment to emphasize the point.

"I don't believe it!"

She tries to initiate an end to the conversation in a civil manner, so that heaven forbid, her friend should not suspect that someone is breathing down her neck.

" *Put down that phone!*"

Again the finger in the air, while the rest of the hand covers the mouthpiece in anticipation of what I will say next. "Yes, Yes," she giggles." I um, yes, but I really have to..."

I cannot wait for a formal ending to the conversation. I do a cartwheel, jump to the ceiling and run around in circles waving my hands.

"**GIVE ME THE PHONE!**"

I think I have her full attention. She covers the mouthpiece.

"Gotta go, Yes. Okay bye, giggle, Okay, yes Okay, yes Okay, bye, yes Okay, yes Okay...bye, yes, I must put down, yes okay, yes okay...."

By the time the phone is available, I am in no frame of mind to call anyone, I forget why I needed the phone in the first place, or the reason I originally needed it is no longer applicable. I ignore the quizzical look on her face, as she wonders why after such a performance I do not even use the phone.

Though the contraption is indispensable and has served me well on many occasions, I loathe telephones. I need a phone if I wish to be part of society. One phone is enough to serve this purpose! I could add another line that may give me access to the outside of my home without having to beg for it, but one phone in the house causes enough havoc. Any more could destroy the family unit.

I foresee what suppertime would sound like. Sheindl, my married daughter calls me. She asks if one of her siblings is available to pick up something from the bakery for her, and oh! by the way, she needs a recipe. I call the family to supper while I look up the recipe. By the time I have finished giving her the recipe no one has yet responded to the supper invitation. I scout around the house and find the rest of the family in various corners with phones attached to their ears. I have to be very innovative to get their attention. I dance the hora while waving freshly baked croissants to entice them.

Their minds are connected through the wires to a voice that is anonymous to me. I am an alien. I look Raizy in the eye. She looks in my direction, but her gaze radiates through me to the wall behind me, and she giggles.

"That is really queer." Raizy says.

I am not offended, because neither the giggle nor her comments are addressed to me. It is something strictly between Raizy, her friend and the telephone satellites.

I would rather steam until I turn into vapor than add yet another telephone line! Even if I could manage to get the family united around the table, with extra phone lines each member will sit ensconced in his or her own world, with the phone glued to the ears. The table conversation could sound something like this.

Shloime: "Mummy can I go out for a half hour before Shmully eats supper?" He watches me turn green and says (into the phone) "My mother said I must eat first. (He covers the mouthpiece and whispers to his mother) Mummy, I am not hungry, can I go play with Shmully now?"

Me. " Absolutely not! Put down the phone before the soup gets cold."

Shlomeh: (into the phone) "My mother says in five minutes." (to mother) "Shmully wants me to go now!"

While I am doling out the soup, Chaya gets a call.

Chaya: "No it is an adjective. Anyway we don't have to do it for tomorrow. Tomorrow it's French and history." Giggle giggle, pause and more giggles. "Oh st-o-o-p, it's just too cute." She takes a beep in the middle, and politely according to my instructions answers "My mother can't come to the phone. She is unavailable."

In the meantime Leah gets an important call. She grabs the cordless.

Leah: "MAZEL TOV! When! Wow!" *Shriek.* " To whom?" *Shriek!* "I don't believe it! " ***Shriek even louder.*** "Excuse me a minute." (turns to me.) "What did you say, Mummy? Yes I finished supper, thank you. I will clear up. (Her index finger points to the ceiling, just as my eyes do. Her eyes x-ray through me to the wall.) You **don't say**! I knew something was going on!" Five more shrieks.

I leave everything alone, and run out for fresh air— with a cell phone that my husband Joseph keeps unused in the drawer for emergencies such as this. I pour out all my venom.

Me: "Hello operator. May the person who came up with the concept of a telephone be blessed with five hundred lines for every relative."

Renovations

Flakes occasionally drop from the ceiling. The floor creaks when you look at it. Under the kitchen counter the raw moldy wood cheekily exposes itself. In short, the house is begging for attention. I really might have done something about the situation a while ago if it were not for Hadassah, my friend and confidante, with whom I speak almost daily. Hadassah is a chronic renovator, but her house is always unfinished.

I recall very well our conversation last Passover. After all the renovations she has gone through, I have yet to see her joy last longer than two months!

"Passover won't cost too much this year," she had said last year. "The children will have a hard time, because their father will find the *afikomen*.." Searching for the *afikomen*, a piece of *matzo* (traditional unleavened bread eaten at Passover), reserved for the end of the meal, is the highlight of the Passover Seder meal for the children. They hide the matzo until their father "discovers" the theft. The matzo must be eaten before midnight, before saying the after meals grace. He searches for it, or makes a deal with the children, who ask for a gift or a privilege such as a later bedtime, before they return the matzo.

"Really? I ask her. "What is the difference between this year and all other years?"

Closets!" answers Hadassah smugly. "We finally had new ones installed after Yanki opened the old ones last Passover. It took us three hours to dig him out from under the books, clothes, blankets shoes, suitcases, photo albums, vacuum cleaner, fans, foldable beds, old typewriters and electric drills and cleansers. With everything in place, Shmulli will easily find the *afikomen* before the children will be able to ask for anything.

"Is it that bad?" I interrupt,

"No, worse," she answers. "It is our only closet. The pullovers lie behind the albums, which are behind the sewing supplies. The blankets were over the shoes, and you should see what happens if someone needs something in hurry!"

"I am really glad you are building closets," I empathize. "It must be very difficult to organize without space."

"The hand-me-downs that I stored away for the next child are always outgrown when I find them. The Purim holiday costumes cannot be found until the holiday is over. Just think of all the things that I have discarded over the years, which I could have accommodated in my new closets. The pickling jars, the baskets, the arts and crafts supplies..."

"Space is great, I know, but please!" I interrupt. "You make it sound as if closets are going to turn your life around."

"It certainly will. With closets I now have everything," she sighs dreamily. "Ah, to sit and admire a neat and tidy closet. I even turned the couch around to face it, so that when I or anyone else wishes to relax, I just open the doors and gloat."

Hadassah's fixation with the closet does not sit well with me. It is before Passover and I have more to do than feed her obsession. I hang up speculating about how long her enthusiasm will last. I remember her ecstasy the year before, when she bought new appliances— a second freezer, two ovens and a dishwasher. Six months later she was fed up with cooking and baking. Her freezer was empty, but she had no more excuses for not being able to bake cheesecake, since she now had a separate oven for dairy food.

When I speak to Hadassah four weeks before Passover, I ask her.

"How are things? It must be so much easier cleaning for Passover with more closet space."

"Space? Isn't that somewhere near the moon?" she says with more than a hint of sarcasm.

I cannot believe my ears.

"But, I mean, didn't you say you were getting closets?"

"Closets, shmozets!" she snaps. "I had so much space that I bought a few linens, T-shirts, books, this and that, and before you know it, I had to put up a sign on the door handles 'DANGER! OPEN AT YOUR OWN RISK'."

"So you can move the couch back. That would save space." I console her.

"I am having a new washroom installed for Passover," Hadassah immediately resumes her bubbly stance. "Can you imagine?! No more lines waiting for the shower and the hair dryer. The little ones will be able to go to bed an hour earlier," she rants and raves about the wonderful change this development will make to her future.

"I am really happy for you," I cheer her on as I share the news of her good fortune.

I hang up and survey my own house. It really could use a facelift. I have graduated to the stage of thinking about it. In the meantime, before I undertake the expense and the trauma of a house under repair, I wait

for Hadassah to prove to me that her renovation has
improved her life for more than three days...

Chicken Soup for America

World leaders are easy to recognize. They wear either business suits with sharply-pressed creases in their pants, or they wear army fatigues. Their manner of speech is the language of a Rhodes Scholar, or gutter slang, depending on whether they govern in a democracy or an autocracy. They do not have too much time to work since it interferes with dinners, meetings and press conferences. I have yet to see a world leader wear an apron or rubber gloves, or pose with a dust mop in the hand. They never say things that warm the heart, like "Oh sweet mother" (*oy mameh zeeseh!*) or "a blessing on your head" (*a brocho oif dain kop!*). All they ever talk about is weapons, money and taxes.

Any good homemaker will tell you that a messy house needs a good cleanup. A messy world is no different. If homemakers were in power, hunger would be passé, everyone would get a fair share of pocket money (as long as they behave properly), and the air would be clean and fresh. The only reason a homemaker is not in power is because she works so hard. There is no time to primp for a camera so she will not be as photogenic as a president sitting in a large office surrounded by paintings of famous men.

Imagine a utopian world where the imaginary Mrs. Kluger might have been the perfect presidential candidate. Mrs. Kluger is a short, frail woman who has managed a family of fourteen people (not including the thirty-two guests her husband brings home from synagogue to join their Sabbath meal every week). It all runs as smoothly as a well-greased cookie sheet. If she had been President, she would have had the United States of America sailing along like a breeze. She never ran for the presidency because she just could not go around shaking people's hands when her hands were sticky with challah dough.

Better yet, imagine if Mrs. Kluger had been Bill Clinton's babysitter when people still thought Little Rock was just a pebble! Our Mrs. Kluger would have been able to brief President Clinton like no one else...

Before Bill Clinton leaves for the White House, he pays a visit to his former babysitter. Mrs. Kluger briefs the future President in her own unique way, knowing, as every good homemaker (*balabusta*) does, that the best way to get a message across is through a well-fed tummy—and there are few who can compare with Mrs. Kluger's culinary expertise. She tries to reassure Bill Clinton as he bites his nails and contemplates the huge responsibility looming before him.

"Now, now, you'll be okay. Listen, you have three things going for you already, and you are not even officially a president yet. First, you are young and healthy, and that's a good start. Presidency is not the best thing for your health. Second, you know how to maneuver and contrive."

"Please don't bring that up again," protests Billy tiredly. "I avoided the army only because I did not believe that America should be fighting in Vietnam..."

"Of course, *Tatteleh*," says Mrs. Kluger. "I remember you in diapers. You always ran when there was trouble. I don't believe in fighting either. Look Billy, what I am saying is that whatever your reason, you wangled out of every accusation, with diplomacy. Every *balabusta* knows that if you cannot take care of your own skin, how will you run the house?"

"What about number three?" asks Billy, eager to change the subject.

"Number three? Well ..." Mrs. Kluger breaks into a smile, "you like broccoli. It's good for you, it's good for the farmers, and it's good for America. If people would eat broccoli instead of smoking cigarettes and drinking alcohol, then three-quarters of the world's problems would be solved. Of course broccoli is not half as good for you as my chicken soup."

"Your chicken soup …it's the greatest," agrees Bill Clinton as he licks his lips. "But America is deep enough in hot soup, I think."

Luckily Mrs. Kluger does not hear. The washing machine is running and she is too busy trying to untangle her grandchild from the telephone cord.

"Remember always, Billy, that there is nothing as good as home-made stuff. It is healthier and cheaper. If you eat out too much, you will eventually be poisoned."

"You are probably mad at me for eating sushi in Japan. I know it isn't kosher but I'm not obligated to eat only kosher …and by the way I didn't really eat it because I can't eat anything that wriggles on my plate. Nothing beats your *gefilte* fish Mrs. Kluger," he adds as appeasement.

Mrs. Kluger raises her hand in protest. "That is not what I mean Billy. I just think America should make more of her own stuff, and not live for Toyotas, Hondas, Sanyo or Seiko. No one can afford to eat out too much. "Here," she says gently, "won't you try my home-made blintzes?"

"Mmmn," murmurs Clinton after every bite. "If

only General Motors were this appealing."

"Waste not, want not," says Mrs. Kluger smugly doling out her nuggets of advice with relish (the sour pickle kind). "I used a whole bottle of sour milk for these blintzes."

"Sour milk?" says Clinton, turning slightly green as he coughs up the piece of blintz that suddenly will not go down his throat.

"And what's more," she adds, "If you heed my advice, then the U.S. should use her own resources too. We would have a lot less taxes to pay."

"You get things for your taxes," Clinton argues, already sounding like a president. "Education, roads, social services..."

"Huh! What social services?" argues Mrs. Kluger incredulously. "Then why is being sick such a luxury? Who can afford to be treated for a really good pneumonia?"

"You don't know anything about running a country," says Clinton, quite irritated at being outsmarted by a perky woman of four-foot-six. "You talk about things like chicken soup and chocolate cake. I, as future president, have greater things on my mind like education, nuclear reactors, iron and steel, and natural resources."

Mrs. Kluger pulls herself up to her full height, stares straight ahead, and with eyes level to the last button of his jacket, she replies: "Excuse me, young man. If anyone taught you a thing or two, it was I. This is a democracy and I can state my opinion. I have, deliver us from the Evil Eye (*bli ayin hore*), twelve children, and well-educated, mind you, on the salary of a caretaker of the synagogue (*shamesh*) plus by babysitting. I have seventeen grandchildren, and you should see them. My son's first child..." and with her fingers she throws a kiss in the air. "Smart as the world (*klieg vi der velt!*) You know what..."

Clinton does know but does not want to hear. He would rather have a war with Iraq any day, than listen to Mrs. K. ramble on about her grandchildren.

"As I was saying," he interrupts "about nuclear energy..."

"Yes! Yes," nods Mrs. K. with enthusiasm, "I use that new clear spray for the bathroom. It's wonderful. It smells better than Mr. Clean."

"N-u-c-l-e-a-r," corrects Clinton. "Like in nuclear bombs," he tries to sound impressive. "It could kill many people."

"You are exaggerating," she laughs. "I love your sense of humor. Anyway I always keep it away from the children, and what you say about iron and steel—we should employ more people to make bars for jails for all those gangsters running loose."

"Mrs. Kluger!" Clinton is horrified. "This is a

democracy, we don't lock people up just like that. We have justice and rights for all races, for all colors, and for all religions."

"Rights!" shrieks the little lady. "My house would be a jungle if I gave my twelve children equal rights. You know why I have such wonderful children Billy," she glares at him. "It's because they have obligations! Everyone is different. I can't make my Motty study. I cannot get my Yossy to stop studying. Pinky is overweight so I feed him less. Ruchi can eat a mountain and you would not know. Berel is ..."

Clinton can barely restrain his annoyance. Here he is about to become President of the United States, and his former babysitter is still treating him like a baby.

"Mrs. Kluger, please stop comparing this diverse country to a nursery. There is so much to contend with, so many groups lobbying for something else. You have no idea."

Mrs. Kluger cuts him short. "Listen *boychik*. If anyone knows about lobbying, it's me. I've been lobbied for the past forty years. Yitszak wants a bike. Sara wants a pajama party. Rachel wants her sister's lunch. Yaffa lobbies to avoid doing the laundry, and I ... could use a rest in Florida ...." she adds with a sigh. Clinton notices that her wrinkles are as creased as the pleats of his pants.

"What you need is more broccoli," says Clinton

sympathetically, proud that for once he is the one doling out the advice. He thanks Mrs. Kluger for her hospitality and bids her farewell as he heads to his limousine to be briefed once more by people in expensive suits who are more photogenic.

Clinton did not heed Mrs. Kluger's valuable advice and not much has changed from presidents who came before and after him. We can only hope for the sake of the world that people will wake up and realize that the best thing for the welfare of the world would be to recognize that homemade chicken soup is the real answer to our woes.

Computer's Revenge

The computer sits royally on the desk in my room, thumbing its fonts at me while I sit with a sheet of paper, chewing my pen between sentences. It is enjoying its sweet revenge for the criticism and sarcasm with which I have attacked technology in the past.

I invested in a computer, hoping it would help me with my increasing workload. There is only so much that I can accomplish with an old à-la-nineteenth-century-style typewriter. I hope to eliminate hours of unnecessary work by having immediate access to an eraser, dictionary, editing, spacing and printing—all at the click of a mouse.

Of course, I do not acquiesce to the temptations of the computer so easily. Eager to take advantage of its benefits, I think that I will easily take control and eliminate the features that would tie me down or distract me. I put the computer in my room, to be used solely at my discretion, ready to fulfil my assignments and deadlines dutifully, skilfully, speedily and in peace.

Little do I know that computers have a mind of their own! My computer and I are just not compatible. It is much easier to pamper a struggling baby and enforce bedtime for ten children than mess around with an arrogant computer that knows it is dealing with an ignoramus.

Computers are supposed to simplify our lives, and they are meant to be easy to access. Meeting the computer for the first time was as strange as being introduced to a Pakistani *Hassid*. In fact, the first time I heard about the word 'icon' I thought that it meant idol worship. After playing around with the computer I am beginning to wonder if that is not the truth.

I press the first button, and Mr. Computer and I make our introductions. The more I click the mouse, the more coded expletives come sputtering out at me. When my daughter explains that the blinking line is not winking to me, but it is simply a "cursor," I realize then that the relationship between the foul-mouthed box and myself needs immediate therapy. I do not take well to curses.

It takes a while to gather courage to be alone with my computer. I keep repeating to myself, "Sticks and stones can break my bones, but words can never hurt me." Then I experiment by clicking on the mouse, creating new files and monsters with titles like XnA/ PwI@***. I almost cause failure in the computer's inner organs.

It takes about thirteen hours of fruitless clicking, until I become adept at unwittingly creating icons, with titles like "mishkebable" or "oszt a kutya faya nekki," and throwing them into the cute recycling bin in the desktop corner. I become so good at this that I feel like a computer whiz.

After another thirty-two hours trying to undo whatever I did, and giving up, I decide it is time to get started on a story, which is why I bought the computer in the first place. I begin typing, but the screen ignores me completely, or snaps back statements like "incorrect file" or "Warning! This machine will explode unless you press XYZ///." The "Help" button is coming loose from my constant pounding, and I am flooded with enough information to become a computer programmer (*if I could only understand it*), but I still have no idea how to get my story onto the screen. I can change the background pattern. I can make the screen smaller or larger. I can choose the colors for the screen saver, but I have no idea how to be productive (in a technological, rather that in the biological way).

By now I have logged 384 hours of experimentation, blockages and temper tantrums and have blamed my husband for every problem from varicose veins to the look of the computer, until he forces me to choose between him or the computer. I then consult for 392 hours with my (ex) friend, begging her on the phone, to explain again how to become unstuck. It is a pity that just when I think I am getting the hang of it, her phone is disconnected. Her new number is unlisted.

I try, I really try, to make the thing work for me. I swallow my pride and gather the nerve to purchase the book *Windows for Dummies*. The sales clerk's smirk when I tell him it is for a friend does not go unnoticed. Flipping through the book, my confidence sinks to an all time low. It has a language of its own. I try to laugh at the cute comments by the author, like "Don't you wish that losing weight was as easy as Minimizing?" I was not encouraged.

It is not easy to admit that after raising a family, doling out advice, tending to the sick, preparing for holidays for so many years, and making the most delicious *kugel* in the neighborhood, or maybe in the world, that…I am, after all, worse than illiterate. I have yet to aspire to the level of a dummy.

So here I am, after having invested time and money in a fancy computer, sitting chewing on my pen and scribbling on paper. So far, all I have from my computer is material for this story, which I will proceed to write with my pencil.

When the RAM Went Wild

After some years, I have finally grown comfortable with my computer. It has served me well, and we have done many stories together. By now, my computer is as ancient as a computer can be. It took a while for me to grasp the differences between a typewriter and a computer and even longer for the computer to get used to me.

We argue a little, computer and I, but it is more of a communication problem than personal differences. I learned to communicate in computer language. There are a few scenes that I am not proud to remember, such as when I was exasperated that this supposedly smart machine could be so utterly stupid. When I finally grasp its mentality (or lack of it), like a little lamb, it lets me take control.

By now I know that all I need to do is press the right keys, and the computer performs. Our teamwork is excellent. I still feel nostalgic about the many stories over which we collaborated together. Unfortunately the ending to the story of my first computer is not "…and they lived happily ever after."

It is a shock to me when after three years of faithful service the computer rebels. The first time it happens is when I press the toolbar, and for a fraction of a second my request teasingly is fulfilled only to disappear into the abyss. From this moment, I can never predict what my computer is going to do next. Suddenly my screen is transformed into a chaotic void. Things I have not asked for appear unexpectedly, and the things I do ask for are totally annihilated in the bowels of the computer. Files evaporate, and the computer flashes warnings like "*You have performed an illegal activity!*" or "*What happened to the World Trade Center is just a tickle compared to what I have in store for you!*"

It consistently threatens to lose my files, shut itself down or blow itself up, blaming me for everything that goes wrong. With each click of the mouse I am warned, threatened and punished by having something vanish. I fear that sooner or later it will inform the police about my criminal behavior.

I am by nature the typical Jewish Mamma—always guilty until proven a little bit less guilty. By the time I realize that *I* am not the problem, but that the obnoxious computer is suffering a mental breakdown, important files I had created years ago have disappeared from the face of the earth.

I call my serviceman five times a day for advice. "Why does my computer not bring up the files I ask for? Why does it blink? Why does it tell me that my files are *read only?* I cannot edit a *read only* file."

"Most probably the computer is working on something. It is still thinking and cannot bring up the file until it has finished with the other project." He answers with authority.

So, my computer becomes a deep thinker in its old age. To me it sounds more like Alzheimer's.

"I need a slave, not a philosopher." I protest. "What can I do?"

When my communication with the serviceman reaches a rate of one call every three minutes, he takes the time to come and check things out. After thirty seconds of juggling around on the keyboard, he tells me that it is the ram.

Huh! So, my little lamb had turned into a RAM! Like a bull in a china shop, a ram in my computer is running wild and tearing up my precious files.

"There is something wrong with the RAM!" he reiterates, seeing that I do not quite get it.

"What are beasts doing in my computer anyway?

142

Get rid of the *it*."

"Without a RAM your computer is scrap metal, madam. Your brain is damaged!"

"Did you come here to give me a diagnosis, or to fix my computer?" I cannot refrain from shouting. "I called for help, not for verbal abuse."

"I mean the computer brain, madam. The RAM is the brain. There are some damaged chips in there."

"I never ate near the computer, and I am allergic to potatoes, so don't tell me it was my fault." I argue as I brace myself for a hefty bill.

The serviceman begins a monologue of technical jargon like bytes and gigabytes. These are numbers with so many zeros following them that scribbled on a pad they look like soap bubbles.

Another thirty seconds of messing around on the keyboard, he nods his head as if he has just discovered the missing links to DNA. "Yes" he says with the earnestness of a doctor diagnosing a fatal disease, "Your computer is badly damaged."

"That is exactly what I told you in the first place." I interject.

The longer the serviceman sits the more expensive the whole situation becomes. My monitor needs so much adjustment that we decide on a new monitor. My keyboard has failings, and we decide a new keyboard is the best thing for it, and if I need some life in this computer, then a new RAM is essential.

The less I understand about what the serviceman is talking about, the more I am ready to pay. All I want is a computer to write a decent story without doing any fancy aerobics to waste my time. He takes my computer away, and like a messenger of doom, he promises to try to salvage as many files as he can, warning me not to expect too much.

With the computer out it is as if a member of the family has disappeared. The more I miss the computer, the more literary inspiration flits through my mind. Ideas surface like pollen dust, but I have become unaccustomed to scribbling on old-fashioned pieces of paper, besides there is never an available pen in my house when I need one. While my computer is being repaired great manuscripts write themselves in my head without being recorded and are lost forever to mankind. However, I do get more housework done.

Instead of allowing my old computer to undergo major brain surgery, I replace it with another, more docile RAM, and chips that do not crumble apart, taking my stories with them. The monitor is a slightly later model. Though my equipment still lags fifteen years behind, for me it is as if I have arrived in the twenty-fifth century. My screen is larger and easier to read. My updated Windows program is more sophisticated and user-friendly.

My files cannot be retrieved! Since this incident, I have lost my faith in the computer. It has lost its charm. The computer may flash at me all of its new updated features, but it is only a tramp covered in makeup. It is all bluff.

I make a mental note never to get too comfortable with computers and backup documents at least ten times. I write one hundred times (actually I type it once and copy one hundred times).

"My computer is not my buddy."

"My computer is not my buddy"

"My computer is not my buddy...

Just as Freud believed that every man/woman has a beast inside, I now know that I must always be one step ahead of the beast (or RAM) that drives my computer.

Women's Communication Network

Telecommunication is quick and expansive. Limitless innovations speed up access to information. There is barely a need for introductions. Your file is in the computer of every department store in which you have ever shopped. Diaper company congratulations are in the mailbox three minutes before your baby is born. Advertisements and brochures drive you to neurosis, trying to prove that you need everything that exists on this planet, always at a very special price.

All you want to know and everything you would rather not is processed directly into your brain, until the cacophony of information and disinformation blends into one big mush, and you yearn to be blissfully ignorant. Account numbers, social security, telephone, credit cards. Guard them with your life, because these numbers squiggle like a snake and can easily end up taking you for a ride.

All the numbers and dates whether cell phones, hotel rooms, EZ passes, laundry labels, transactions and interactions, and overreactions are recorded and ready to embarrass you when they come forth to remind you some day of something you did in your past. From these evolve statistics and more information such as whether you and your spouse are compatible, or whether you will make it in business, and what your children will amount to. Communication experts are brazen enough to even take credit for this.

In fact, the real designers of the most reliable information system have never been legitimately acknowledged. It dates back thousands of years when the second woman on earth was born. Women have created a foolproof system of communication that is still as effective today as ever, with an added ingredient of human intrigue that computers will never have.

While computer methodology is based on rules of ratiocination, the Women's Communication Network (wcn) is based on the concepts of feelings, tastes, personal opinions, humour, compassion, the weather and 'how are you feeling today?' It is an infinitely more colorful and exciting system than the one conjured up by the geniuses sitting in stuffy offices with their brains electronically wired to their computers.

The full potential of WCN has never been recognized because it lacks the promise of financial gain, it is not job-creative, and it is too obvious and natural. If the WCN charged for their services, the telecommunication experts could easily be declared humbug, but if the WCN were a business it would never be so effective. The most enhancing features of WCN are its spontaneity and its changeability.

Even without pressing a button the WCN has the right information. It comes forth impromptu, any place and any time. There is also no stop button, a minor handicap on such occasions as when planning a quick supper of a hot dog sandwich. There is sure to be some member of the WCN ready to inform you that hot dogs are loaded with monosodium glutamate and carcinogens that will likely kill your family.

The information spews forth like a fountain located wherever two women meet. All you have to do is drink it. Scouting for a doctor, a dentist, or a butcher? Tune in to WCN and you will laugh and cry at the horror stories, success stories and anecdotes on the topic.

Computers can't see you. They need to be supplied with numbers to assess whether you are fat or thin. Five foot two and two hundred pounds is overweight. Lose twenty pounds and the computer still considers you overweight. It will never congratulate you and tell you how much better you look, nor will it notice rings under your eyes, worry about you, or offer to take care of your children for a day.

A typical WCN case is when I join the line at the check-out counter at the local hardware store. The queue becomes a WCN forum when two women get into an exchange of profound ideas and thoughts. One lady describes in depth the ups and downs of renovating her kitchen. Three heads behind me another member of the Network is avidly jotting down the information, and piping in with even more creative ideas and information. They are so innovative that I notice yet another person scribbling down notes on the back of her prescription receipt.

"Excuse me, are you ready?" asks the checkout lady with a nervous cough.

"Ceramic floors are slippery," continues the speaker, addressing the person in line behind her, oblivious to the cashier. I notice one customer in the check-out line return some ceramic tiles she is holding to the shelf.

The cashier jingles her bracelets. "Uh hum!"

"Blue? I don't think blue goes with the rust as well as green would."

The cashier stretches out her cough to give it more emphasis.

"By the way, how is Moishe since you stopped feeding him peanut butter. It worked miracles for Mechel!"

The next customer firmly disagrees, but the one near the cash is adamant, and initiates a lively dialogue about nuts. This evolves into a discussion about the high prices of food, and ends with a discourse about the coming elections. The sore-footed customers are also treated to a wealth of information on ways and means to get Medicare to pay for orthopaedic shoes.

"MOVE AHEAD PLEASE!" Exclaims Madam Cough-a-Lot rather sharply.

Such ingratitude! The WCN did not even charge for all those money-saving, life-saving, and time-saving nuggets of information on decorating and life in general. It is obvious that not everyone appreciates the system.

Even the doctor with the full waiting room can attribute his success to the WCN. It is universally recognized that a body was created to fight against invading germs. Sniffles generally disappear even without any doctor's intervention. The doctor's office is the recharge center for the Women's Communication Network. There is always a coffee klatch in the waiting room. The doctor advises patients to rest, drink fluids, take antibiotics, exercise, stop working, stop eating, and to come back next week. Most people know this even before they come. Every woman is a qualified member of the international Women's Communication Network. The women in the waiting room will provide you with the real remedies— garlic juice, olive oil, lemon tea, bracelets to protect against the evil eye, prayers, recipes for puff pastry and the latest market listings of where you are likely to find the cheapest prices for cabbage and paper towels. All this information and more are supplied to you while you wait to get into the examination room.

Nothing can replace the WCN. The baby food company might welcome you home from hospital with coupons for baby products, but the WCN information will ensure that your family will have a Sabbath meal ready before you come home. A computer will calculate and store information, but never will it understand you, laugh with you, cry with you or treat you as a comrade—as does the WCN.

Squeezing in a Succah

Succoth, the holiday of remembrance of the Jewish exodus from Egypt and their travel through the desert, has been over for a while. The crudely-built wooden structures (the *succahs*)—that were erected to commemorate the sojourn of the Jews in the desert while living under the protection of the clouds—are being dismantled. The little huts perched on the balconies of the houses in the city of Outremont during the holiday of Succoth with their roofs of bamboo and ferns have all been packed away. That is, *almost* all!

One structure remains, much to the chagrin of many of the non-Jewish Outremont dwellers who are accustomed to a city that is as well groomed as the poodles and pedigreed canines that they elegantly lead around the streets. To a practicing Jew, a *succah* is beautiful, not for its structure but for the joy of the festival that it represents, and all the traditional details that revolve around it. Looked at only with the eye, and without the heart, this particular *succah* is a real klutz. If it stands around a few days longer, there are sure to be complaints from neighbors whose sensitive tastes cannot tolerate any impairment to the aesthetic air of this elite neighborhood.

After Succoth, even a Jew would not suspect that the above-mentioned structure is actually a *succah*. It looks more like a tent for camping out, or perhaps a tarpaulin covering a snow blower or a tank. Fabricated from strips of white vinyl stapled together, the thing flaps over the porch in the wind. The reason this succah still stands is because it is not just a run-of-the mill *succah*. This *succah* was a community effort shared by many learned sages, and Talmudic students, and the collective expertise of ordained rabbinical clergy in Montreal and New York. The mastermind of this *succah* is not about to dismantle the succah before the forthcoming visit by his father from New York. He is very proud of it and wants him to see it.

I do not have at my fingertips the fine points and complex rules for Succoth, nor do I profess to understand the technical part of this particular "learned succah" (*lomdishe succah*) I can only relate the female version of the story, because this *succah* is the property of my daughter Sheindl, and her husband Shulem, and

I have the story from her.

Credit for this *succah* comes to Sheindl, who lives in an apartment building with a long but narrow balcony that is partly covered by an overlapping beam, leaving, in my estimation, about eighteen inches of uncovered balcony that could serve for the roof of the *succah* (which must be open to the sky). Having small children, Sheindl suggested that this year they needed a *succah* of their own. Schlepping the children to her parents' house for every meal would be very tiresome for the children and mess up their sleeping schedules. Moving in for the holiday of Succoth is impossible, since we would already be hosting three of our other children with their families. When they arrive, then the seven children I still have at home develop five more personalities each. When the family gets together, the combination of children with their nieces and nephews is something like a Molotov cocktail in a box of matches.

Since the New Year six weeks ago, my daughter keeps phoning at one-hour intervals to update me. The formulated plans are activated only two days before Succoth, when Shulem begins scrounging around for supplies, and for leftover beams from someone else's old *succah*. They are outgrowing their apartment, and it is not worth investing in something grand, since moving is imminent. Shulem finally assembles the materials that patiently await their fate on the balcony, while Sheindl impatiently prods her husband, reminding him that Succoth is only one day away, and it is not too early to begin. Shulem's search for a suitable *esrog* and *lulov* (a combination of a particular lemon-like fruit and a palm branch, over which special blessings are made during the holidays) is still under way, and he is too preoccupied to even gather the tools.

The day before the holiday, and in a panic, Shulem, never a handyman by nature, realizes that building a *succah* does not just involve randomly banging in nails. Sheindl tries to maintain an air of calm as she struggles to keep the children out of her husband's way as he sweats over its construction.

"How is the *succah* coming along?" I keep calling for an update.

"I don't know if we will have one or not, as yet." Sheindl answers with an affected calmness that sets my heart pounding. I have a vested interest. Without their *succah,* I anticipate an additional family of six joining our repast. That is no problem in itself, I can always add some vegetables or fish into my twenty-quart pot— but I worry whether or not my balcony is sturdy enough, and how to stretch the table and floor space.

Sunset, the official start to the holiday, begins at six o'clock, after which all work must be put aside. Sheindl continues washing, wiping, and dusting, and occasionally untangling the children who take advantage of their gratuitous freedom. At one o'clock Shulem is still sorting out which piece of wood belongs where.

By three o'clock with the help of neighbors the *succah* is up, and Sheindl shares with me a sigh of relief, and whoops in celebration. The young men on the porch study their masterpiece and become involved in a discussion of some tracts of Talmud that deal with the legalities of a *succah*. Sheindl prefers that they discuss it somewhere else to give her a chance to put the finishing touches to the holiday preparations. The debate intensifies by the minute. Soon the books are dragged out from Shulem's bookshelves, and with tools in one hand, they page through them with the other. Sheindl's suspicions are soon confirmed when a flustered Shulem drops his tools, declaring he is going to the *dayan* (an ordained rabbi who is consulted when Talmudic issues arise) with the blueprint of his succah.

"There are some questions involved," he tells Sheindl gently as if expecting an outburst. With three hours to the holiday it is not the time for Sheindl to begin learning about Talmudic legalities. All she really wants to know at this moment is whether or not the children should nap, in case they have to come to our house for the evening meal.

The next hour is a flurry of events. The *succah* as erected is rendered not kosher. The *dayan* is researching whether a kosher *succah* on a porch of such limited dimensions is possible, and also other questions that came up in his research. Though he has been a *dayan* for over thirty five years, this *succah* is a fresh challenge. There are many Talmudic legalities involved. He confers with rabbis in the city and overseas, while Shulem runs home to dismantle the contraption that is declared *not* a *succah*. Two hours before sunset, the *dayan* himself, accompanied by Talmudic students with Shulem and his friends tagging behind, come to study the *succah*, and figure out how it can be constructed in a way that would render it kosher.

An endless succession of curious scholarly sightseers marches back and forth through the dining room as Sheindl tries to do and redo preparations for the holiday.

At first Shulem is about to throw in the towel and forget about having their own *succah* this year. "Your mother makes delicious matzo balls anyway," he comforts Sheindl. As the tension grows around the succah it becomes a challenge. Shulem's despair turns to determination, and the *succah* becomes a mission...

His friends arrive from all directions with new supplies, and as word spreads about his unusual *succah*, more and more opinions and suggestions spew forth, and more and more helpers come, making him more and more dizzy. Half an hour to sunset, and by now the wives of his friends are sending search dogs to sniff out the location of their husbands and remind them that they are needed at home.

Sheindl lights the candles exactly ten minutes after Shulem throws the last tool into the tool box, and places a small white tablecloth over the precarious raw wooden home-made contraption that is attached to the balcony and looks more like a high chair than the table it is meant to be.

Shulem's newly-married brother-in-law, Srully knocks on the door. He is ready for the holidays in full regalia with his silk coat and fur hat (*shtreimel*), holding the traditional palm branch in one hand. He calmly asks Shulem if he has time to weave the rings for the basket with the four herbs with which the lulov comes. Shulem groans, as he glances at the ticking clock as if it is a bomb about to explode.

"I was figuring on *your* help with my *lulov*," he exclaims.

Procrastination is a genetic feature in the family. Sheindl can barely refrain from laughing (and crying).

Through some miracle, Shulem is in the synagogue with perfect timing, and he expends his built-up adrenalin on his prayers. The *dayan* greets him with a knowing smile, and makes a request that Shulem feels is equivalent to being ordained to the highest order of the kingdom.

"Can I come over tomorrow and make *kiddush*

(blessing over wine and sweets) in your *succah!*"

This Succoth, Shulem and Sheindl own the world. The eve of the holiday is best forgotten, but this holiday will be recorded for eternity.

As I've already said, I am no Talmudic scholar. To me this *succah* is the oddest looking one I have ever seen. It has crooked beams, and a string along the edge of the branches that cover the roof. The succah cannot be made of wood because the thickness of the wood would render the space in the *succah* narrower than the minimum allowed according to Jewish law (*halacha*). Shulem had purchased vinyl, which he wrapped over the porch railings. Every odd detail has some explanation that sends the men into lively discussion of these rarely-used halachic adjustments. There is one succah decoration hanging from the beam on the ceiling and one on the wall, for aesthetic value. To Sheindl they are the most beautiful works of art. Her children had worked hard on them in nursery school and kindergarten.

The *succah* will soon be dismantled. It is amazing how beautiful something so technically coarse could be. There is no way that the neighborhood of Outremont will accept the *thing* as anything but trash. Eight days of this eyesore is too much. But to the owners of this *succah*, it has special qualities and the holiday is just too short.

An Open Invitation

The Sanders are great socialites. They are well-beloved and they love everyone. This never should have been, nor was it a problem, until the wedding of their daughter, Sima. Neither the reception hall nor their budget is half as big as their hearts, and they can barely accommodate their extended family, let alone all their friends.

From the day of her engagement, until four weeks before the wedding they wrangle over the guest list. They borrow the mailing lists from the various community organizations. Only one name is eliminated, and even that is after a fiery argument between husband and wife.

"I remember sitting next to her on a chartered bus two years ago, and we had such a nice conversation,"

Mrs. Sander argues. "She will be really insulted if we do not invite her."

They go through all the Hassidic directories for Europe and North America, eliminating one half the listings less three. Sima declares she will never be able to face people in the future. Mr. Sander's reasoning that Simeleh would never meet, let alone recognize, those people in her lifetime is no consolation.

Simeleh has circles under her eyes as she works on her list late into the night. With every passing month the list grows and grows, until it contains more pages than the twenty-nine Talmudic volumes of *Shas* on the bookshelf. The Sanders slowly begin to realize that this is way out of hand.

They roll up their sleeves and start to eliminate. The first group to be tossed is those who they have neither seen nor spoken to in the past five years. When they realize that this includes half of their relatives, they make exceptions. The next bunch to cut off is relatives dating back to more than eight generations, unless in the meantime they have come back through marriage into the family.

Mr. Sander is a well-known supporter of all kinds of institutions and of all rabbis. Every name in the directory with the title rabbi attached is invited. After more careful analysis of the list, Mr. Sander realizes that in the directories, not only rabbis, but also shoemakers, comedians (*batchonim*), plumbers and carpenters are also designated rabbis. The family spends two evenings ferreting out the true-blue rabbis from the shoemakers, plumbers and carpenter rabbis. The non-*rebbishe* rabbis (whose parents were not rabbis) who have become family within the recent eight generations are privileged to remain on the list. The list shrinks to the size of the commentaries on the Talmud.

As the wedding expenses mount, the Sanders find the list is still too long, and time is getting short. They sit together, dissecting their community, their friends and their relatives. Mrs. Sander is torn asunder at having to cut drastically from the forty-five ladies in her swimming group.

"Okay, well Etty Segal, I *have to* invite, because we always share a taxi. Zissy; *her I have to invite.* She nearly drowned when I dived right on top of her. Tsurty, no question!" She only manages to eliminate one lady. "But *I can't* make an exception out of one person, *so I have to* invite her too," she reasons.

Finally, she is convinced to invite only those who have children of the same ages, and with whom she has sat at a recent affair. It all boils down to only one person being eligible to attend the grand affair.

Six weeks before the wedding the list is the size of a set of holiday prayer books.

"Still too much," Mr. Sander declares, while he juggles figures on his electronic organizer, making more cutbacks. He whittles down the list of the members of the three synagogues he attends, to include only where he prays on the Sabbath. When that amounts to three hundred and sixty people, he includes only his aisle, and finally his bench.

Sima's friends are a completely different matter. She cannot find anyone to cut out. It takes coaxing and prodding before she eliminates all the children and parents for whom she was a babysitter. Her list contains everyone she has ever heard about or been in contact with, even through a passing hello. Included are the senior citizens in the three old age homes she visits, as well as all her fellow campers plus the other camps against which they played sports. After cajoling, coaxing, and calming her bitter tears, the list is reduced drastically. Five weeks before the wedding, and it is the size of the Psalms.

As the wedding day draws nearer, Mr. Sander realizes that he needs to pull his purse strings even tighter. Wedding related costs keep on spiraling to unreachable proportions. The in-laws are pressing the Sanders to let them know the number of invitations they should print. Three weeks before the wedding, the family has one final session. They cut left, right, and center.

"I am not going to waste sixty cents on a stamp for

the office building doorman," declares Mr. Sander firmly.

"She always makes me wait, even if I am there first," reflects Mrs. Sander, as she draws a line through the name and address of her chiropractor's secretary.

Sima tearfully covers her page with crossings back and forth, up and down.

The great friendships of six months ago dissolve into thin air. At this time, the Sanders become more dependent on their bank accounts than on their friends. Thirteen days before the wedding, the list is no longer than a pocket-sized travel prayer card.

The Sanders look at the list and then at each other.

"This is a joke," exclaims Mrs. Sander. " I want friends, not enemies."

"This is crazy," wails Sima. "I want a wedding (*chasseneh*), not a staff meeting,"

"We have to think of something else. I won't be able to show my face anywhere," mumbles Mr. Sander.

They finally devise a plan that is financially efficient, and that will also enlighten them as to who are their true friends. They will print an invitation in the local papers. This way their friends will decide on the degree of their friendships. Whoever attends is welcome with good feelings all around.

If you see the Sanders invitation hanging in the bakery, just remember how much thought went into it. Since this story has acquainted you with the family, you may even feel close enough to attend. They will be enlightened that they have more friends than they knew. If serving portions fall short, then good friends will always forgive.

Fighting Terrorism in All
Shapes and Sizes

Sheindl my eldest daughter is *almost* flawless. A textbook model mother, and the relationship between her and her husband Shulem has a five star rating. She is tolerant, congenial, and gets along with just about anyone. However, even the finest of people have their limits.

Sheindl faces her test when she is rudely awakened early one morning by a perky little fly buzzing around her ears. It supervises her morning ablutions (*negel vasser*), and follows her to the shower, where it patiently rubs its forelegs on the curtain rod. It unobtrusively hitches a ride on her shoulders as she moves to the kitchen where it gains confidence and attempts to participate in the breakfast preparations.

Like the bombers over enemy territory the fly circles

around Sheindl, landing intermittently on strategic spots—on her head, nose, hands and sleeves. Sheindl obliviously waves it off at each touchdown, too involved with serving the children's breakfast to allow the activity of a mere fly to invade her consciousness. She realizes that she is under attack when her arms became weary from brandishing the butter knife, the tea kettle, or whatever she is holding each time the persistent fly heads towards her. Soon the fly changes course and shuttles back and forth from the cottage cheese to the bread, and almost dares to take a swim in her baby's glass of juice.

Sheindl's gentle nature does not let her harm the creature, even under such dire harassment. She raises the window shades to allow the sunshine to entice the fly to make its escape. The fly is apparently too domesticated and prefers to rub its legs together on the refrigerator to recoup more energy for the next assault. Sheindl then opens the door and gently tries to coax it out with a towel. The fly applies for permanent residency.

Everything on this earth, however mundane it may seem, has a heavenly purpose that we do not always understand.

"This cannot go on," thinks Sheindl "This fly is stalking me. There must be some deeper significance. Perhaps it is a reincarnation from some soul needing atonement." Always ready to help another in need,

Sheindl decides, "I will do a good deed (*mitsvah*) in its merit, and release it from its earthly mission."

Sheindl says all her morning blessings loudly with fervour, with the spiritual future world of the little fly in mind, and at the same time thinking of her own peace in this physical world. The fly expresses its gratitude for Sheindl's consideration by becoming more and more friendly.

Was this fly so evil in its former life that it requires fulfilment of so many good deeds (*mitsvos*) to restore its spiritual balance, or is it sent to irritate Sheindl as an atonement for her own sins? Whatever its mission the *almost* perfect Sheindl's irritation intensifies by the minute.

The fly buzzes in harmony to her blessings over her food, grace after meals, her morning prayers (*shacharis*) and her recitation of psalms (*tehillim*) becoming progressively more attached to her throughout the day.

Sheindl hears the footsteps of her husband Shulem coming up the steps, and she leaps to the doorway and greets him in a faint. His heart misses a beat at the sight of his pale, panic-stricken wife, and he braces himself to come to the rescue.

"Save me!" she sobs in desperation.

He tries to keep a straight face when he hears who is the oppressor. Shulem, who is six-foot-three in his stocking feet, arms himself with a dishtowel and girds himself for hand-to-wing combat. It is a very uneven battle. The fly has the advantage! Shulem tries to coax it out the window, but it sits complacently on the dishtowel obviously enjoying it like the thrill of a roller coaster. Shulem is a little queasy about killing, but the chutzpah of the fly touches a raw nerve, and with all his might, he shakes the fly onto the table and lands the dishtowel on top of it with a smash.

CRASH! Two plates and a cup shatter on the floor. The fly flits triumphantly back and forth in front of Sheindl's eyes. She sends it off onto the counter, where Shulem waits ready in ambush.

"GLOP!" the handle of the soup pot gets caught in the dishtowel and soup splatters out over the edge and onto the floor. The fly dives for the spoils, enjoying the noodles all to itself.

Sheindl runs from the room. She cannot bear to watch her hero defeated by something smaller than a pea. Through her closed door she hears a chair topple over and her husband slip on the spilled soup.

"*Bin Ladin, Get Out!* (*Araus!*)" Sheindl had never heard Shulem speak in that tone, but such is war!

After the maneuvers subside, Shulem finally declares victory. Though he is not privy to finding the body, there is no sign of the fly. Sheindl surveys the collateral damage, and helps pick up the pieces. As she bends over the dustpan while sweeping up the glass, she hears a familiar buzz from a fly that is happy to see her. Fighting terrorism by conventional means just does not work.

After two days of continued regal behavior Sheindl breathes a sigh of relief. The tiny terrorist disappears. Sheindl finally declares her tormentor to be *neutralized*. It is either dead or out of harm's way. Perhaps Sheindl has earned enough merits to restore the fly/soul's good credit in the spiritual realm, or perhaps the fly is not up to living with such elevated company and it is on a new mission seeking to terrorize a place that fosters it. Whichever way, this story goes to prove that the true antithesis to terrorism is not war but spiritual improvement.

My Kreplach Don't Leak Anymore

I have not noticed any drastic changes in myself over the years. There is nothing obvious about my behaviour that would make me say, "Well, look at this, isn't it amazing. I am maturing!" What strikes me is that the average eighteen-year-old is getting progressively younger than in my time, and that youth generally has become more youthful than I can remember ever being.

Other people must notice something about me. When young ladies stand up for me on a bus, I really appreciate it, but I still get this feeling that it is an exaggeration. When I am addressed as Mrs. it does not seem natural. I may be a grandmother but I have not changed one bit since my school days. That is, until recently when my life turned around.

I am preparing cheese-filled dough (*kreplach*) for the holiday of Shavuos as I have been doing for the past twenty-five or so years and, wonder of wonders, my *kreplach* don't leak! I cannot in all honesty tell you what I did differently or better than all other years. All I can attribute to this remarkable achievement is that I have matured. Ask me why my *kreplach* do not leak and I will smile, and knowingly suggest the way my mother did, that "if you press the fork around the edge a little harder, or maybe don't stuff them so much or maybe..." Now that I have my *kreplach* right, I finally understand why my mother could never give me the exact recipe for all her delicious food.

"About a handful of salt and two of sugar, not much oil.... you could try a drop of water.... and if it is still too dry then... see what happens," were the most punctilious details she could offer.

Before, when I set out on any culinary adventure, I reread the recipe twenty-three times, to estimate how difficult it was, or how time consuming. I needed to know the exact order of ingredients, the time needed for mixing, stirring and baking. I deserve some academic recognition for my research into substituting one ingredient for another. Days were spent calculating how to double or halve recipes, and figuring out how much I needed to produce. Between my family and guests, I always had to recalculate how many people would be sharing our meals. Veal bones were measured with a tape measure before I dared add them to a soup. I did breathing exercises to relieve the tension before I poured out my short personal prayers (*techinos*) for the success of whatever I was about to bake, and the well-being of my home, my neighborhood, this world and the next.

My whole approach to life has changed, now that my *kreplach* don't leak any more. Let the whole bus stand up for me. I have become of age. Ask me for advice; I will give you all you ever need to know and more. The space used for my recipe books is being replaced with photo albums of my grandchildren. My adult instincts are reliable enough to bring salvation to soggy dough. I will knead away to my heart's content, adding water, flour, or salt at my own discretion. I am here my child, if you need any help of advice to answer all your queries. I am a mature woman!

"Try adding an egg or two.... I guess if you want to add pepper it won't do any harm."

Many years have passed since my school days. Fear of failure is a youthful phenomenon. It is too late for me to make a first impression. My mother used to tell me that a good cook is not one who never makes mistakes, or whose food is always a perfect success. A good cook is one who has the courage to fix his/her mistakes. This applies to every avenue of life and is the ingredient that separates the child from the adult.

My kreplach don't leak anymore! I have the domestic authority to answer the queries of all you youngsters who study a cookbook with awe.

Even as I yell it out for all the world to hear *"my kreplach don't leak anymore!"* I am taming down a potato salad that turned out a little too spicy. Now there, I will try a little sugar, and carrots won't do any harm. Maybe I will double the potatoes and get rid of the surplus by offering it to supplement Meals-on-Wheels. In the worst case, if it won't be a potato salad, then I will have just created my very own specialty, and another notch in my fast turning wheel of maturity. Please do not ask me for this recipe.

Making perfect *kreplach* is one thing but getting your children to eat them is another! I remember the story my mother told me about a little boy who would not eat *kreplach*. However she tried, she could not induce him to taste even one. One day she decided to show him how *kreplach* are made, sure that he would surely try it once he had seen the ingredients.

She mixed the eggs and flour and sugar and he watched her with interest as she kneaded the dough.

"Yum!" he said. "When will it be ready?"

"Wait,"she said. "First we must make the cheese mixture."

Her son was drooling. "Can I lick a little bit?"

THEN AND o o

"Oh no! You must wait until it is finished," she answered and pretended not to notice him dip his small finger around he edge of the bowl and then lick his finger dry.

"What now?" he asked.

"Now we must roll the dough, and cut it into squares."

The son helped her cut out the squares and before long she was spooning the cheese mixture onto the dough.

"Can't I have just one?" the child asked.

"Not yet," said the mother. "There's just one more thing."

"Soooo lo-ong!" the child complained.

The mother took the first square and folded it over the cheese.

"*Oy vey!*" the child cried. "*Kreplach!* Yuck!"

A Little More Information

Afikomen
At the Passover table there are three matzos. The middle one is broken and the larger half is set aside in an embroidered bag. This larger matzo is the *afikomen* and it must be eaten no later than midnight. The head of the table hides the *afikomen* in the cushion on which he is leaning—the Passover Seder is celebrated with the comfort of cushions to commemorate the freedom of the Jews from slavery. Throughout the long ritual meal the children look for an opportunity when he is not looking to "steal" the matzo. They hide the matzo and at the end of the meal the head of the table "discovers" that the *afikomen* is missing and he searches for it. Not finding it, he barters with the children for its return. The children give their conditions for its return, usually gifts or special privileges.

Cheder
A traditional Jewish primary school that offers religious teaching.

A Day in the Life of a Hassid
Daily life of a Hassid always includes morning prayers, afternoon prayers (usually just before sunset), evening prayers (usually just after sunset), prayers before and after meals, and bedtime prayers. There is ritual washing before getting out of bed, and at other times such as after touching an animal or touching a body part that is normally covered, or after touching something unclean such as a shoe. Men pray in synagogue within a quorum of ten men (a *minyan*); women and children can pray without such a quorum.

Dayan/Dayanim
The head of the rabbinical court of each Hassidic community is a *dayan*. He rules on issues of Jewish law (*Halacha*). He can also be a mediator between disputing parties. He is a scholar of Jewish law with whom rabbis and other members of the community will consult. *Dayans* study for many years and then go through an internship with other *dayanim*. They are ordained by their mentors and are adopted or hired by their community or synagogue.

Dress customs
Hassidic dress customs are the most visible thing we see about the Hassidic community. For holidays and the Sabbath married males wear traditional round fur-trimmed hats (*shtreimel*) and traditional black silk coats (*beketshe*), for which each Hassidic community has its own distinctive style. On other days, men usually wear plain dark suits and white shirts. Women and girls cover their arms and legs modestly and married women cover their hair with a head covering or a wig.

G-d
Religious Jews do not spell out the word G-d out of respect for the Creator. The common name used is *Hashem*, literally, The Name.

Halacha
The *Halacha* is the code of Jewish law. It is a large body of rules and regulations that specify what is permitted and what is forbidden, and it covers all aspects of daily life. For example, it specifies that any kind of work or transportation on the Sabbath is forbidden, including riding in cars and buses, and turning on light switches. The laws are many and they can be very complex, especially how they are to be

interpreted in the modern world. The *dayanim* interpret
the *halacha* and bring it to the level of daily life and practice.

Hassid/Hassidic Community

The meaning of the word Hassid in Hebrew is "pious."
The Baal Shem Tov (circa 1700-1760) established the Hassidic Movement in response to the difficult and repressive
situation in which Jews found themselves in Eastern Europe
at the time. The movement stressed serving G-d with joy
and inspiration and it included singing and dancing as well
as storytelling. Charismatic leadership and joyful ritual
were combined with intellectual and spiritual insights to
appeal to the common Jew who had not previously had
access to Torah learning in traditional Judaism. The Baal
Shem Tov's followers and scholars spread out through
Europe and later through the rest of the world and attracted
adherents from among disillusioned Jews and revered
Torah scholars. Initially there was considerable opposition
to the Movement until it became recognized and established.

Kiddush

A *kiddush* is a ritual that sanctifies a Jewish holiday, the
Sabbath, or a special occasion. It is a blessing over wine or
grape juice that comes before a meal or the serving of sweets/
cake that takes place in a family or in a group. *Kiddush* is
always said before the evening meal that opens the Sabbath
or a holiday, and before the morning meal on the Sabbath.
A ceremonial silver cup is often used for the wine or juice.

Kosher

Kosher literally means "fit" or acceptable. Kosher also
designates the complex dietary laws that are part of the
Halacha. These laws determine the food that observant Jews
are permitted to eat. For example, since milk and meat

181

products must never be mixed, kosher households maintain completely separate systems (plates, cutlery, cooking utensils, pots and pans, etc.) for foods that contain milk and meat products. The dietary laws also forbid the eating of pork and they include prescriptions on how meat should be slaughtered. Hassidic communities practice very strict observance of these laws. In English the term is now also commonly used to loosely describe something that is acceptable or legitimate.

Kugel
A baked pudding, often made with noodles, potatoes or bread, and eggs, with either sweet or savoury ingredients. It is often used as a luncheon side dish or dessert for Sabbath or holiday meals because it can be prepared ahead of time to be eaten later on days when cooking is not permitted.

Kreplach
Kreplach are triangular dumplings filled with seasoned ground meat or cheese. They are made by placing a spoonful of filling in the center of a square of noodle dough, then folding the dough in half diagonally to form a triangle. The edges must be well sealed or the kreplach will leak! Kreplach can be boiled in water and then either fried or added to soup. Sweet cheese kreplach are traditionally served on *Shavuot*. Meat kreplach are served on *Yom Kippur*, the Day of Atonement, *Hoshana Rabbo*, the last day of *Succoth*, and also on *Purim*, the early spring holiday that celebrates the overturn of the decree of the Persian King that allowed the slaughter of the Jews.

Matzo
Matzo is the only bread that is eaten during Passover. It commemorates the Exodus of the Jews from their captivity

in Ancient Egypt. In their hurry to leave they baked their bread before it had time to rise, resulting in matzo. The unleavened Passover matzo is made of only flour and water and baked in strictly prescribed ways, no leavening products of any kind are permitted during the seven or eight days of Passover.

Negel vasser

Negel vasser is the ritual hand washing that is done at different times of the day. Upon awakening, water kept at the bedside is spilled on the hands over a pail or basin and the hands are washed, after which an observant Jew will say a prayer of thanks for allowing him or her to wake up (*modeh ani*). It is a spiritual as well as a physical cleansing. Hands are also washed before eating bread.

Peyos

For Hassidic males the hair from around the temples of the head is traditionally never cut. The hair is formed into *Peyos*, the traditional long sidelocks or curls of hair that Hassidic males wear on either side of the face, or tucked behind their ears.

Physical Contact

Physical and social contact between men and women is not allowed except between children or members of the immediate family. This custom sometimes leads to great misunderstanding and misinterpretation. When Hassidic men and women leave the confines of their home and community they can be faced with uncomfortable situations such as being unable to directly accept change from the hands of a shopkeeper or cashier of the opposite sex, or being unable to shake hands with a member of the opposite sex. It can be even more complicated in situations that might otherwise be considered casual, work, or social exchanges between men and women, or being in enclosed spaces with medical staff of the opposite sex. These situations sometimes require long and complicated explanations on the part of Hassidic men and women. Situations often arise where there is not time, or it is not possible, to provide these explanations and the result can be misunderstanding.

Phylacteries (tefillin in Hebrew)

Phylacteries are two small leather boxes with narrow leather straps attached, that contain Hebrew Scripture written on small parchment scrolls. During prayer these leather boxes are placed on the forehead and on the left arm and they are attached with the leather straps in a carefully prescribed ritual. Phylacteries are required during morning prayer for all Jewish males over the age of thirteen.

Reb

The term *reb* is used as an honorary title of respect for a Hassidic man.

Rebbe

A *rebbe* is a Hassidic spiritual leader who inspires his followers. The Hassidic movement revolves around charismatic *rebbes*, the first of whom was Rebbe Yisroel, better known as Baal Shem Tov, the man of good repute. In the Hassidic community *rebbes* are men of G-d, to whom people gravitate for advice and spiritual leadership. A *rebbe* is not necessarily the rabbi or head of a synagogue but he will always be learned in the Torah (Scripture and commentaries). Hassidic communities develop around individual *rebbes* and on the death of the spiritual leader of a community a son or follower will sometimes take on the role of the *rebbe*. Children also refer to their teachers as *rebbe*.

Shovevim

Shovevim is a six-week period in winter in which the weekly *Torah* readings relate to the time of the Exodus of the Jews from Egypt until they receive the *Torah* from G-d through Moses. During this period study and prayer are more intensive and students especially are expected to make extra efforts in their spiritual studies.

Succah/Succoth

Succoth is the fall holiday commemorating the forty years the Jews spent in the desert under the leadership of Moses. A *succah* is an outdoor construction that is made for the holiday of *Succoth*. A *succah* has no roof since it must be open to the sky in memory of the cloud that followed and protected the Jews during their stay in the desert. The *succah* is loosely covered by leaves or branches and the interior walls are usually decorated with paintings, artwork, crafts, and lights. During the eight days of the holiday all meals are taken in the *succah* and if there is room the men and boys can sleep in it. There are complex rules in the *Halacha* about how and where a *succah* must be constructed.

Talles

A *talles* is a prayer shawl that is used by men during Jewish morning prayers, and for prayers on the Sabbath and certain Jewish holidays. It has special fringes attached to the four corners. The *talles* is a very personal item and it is usually carried to the synagogue in a small special bag.

Tsadik /Tsadikim

Tsadikim are righteous people who devote themselves to spiritual life and who have reached a very high level of spirituality and communion with G-d. A *tsadik* is not necessarily a rabbi or a community leader though he often is. A *tsadik* can sometimes intervene with G-d on behalf of others because of his strong connection to Him.

Yeshiva
A *yeshiva* is a Jewish secondary school for Talmudic and rabbinical studies.